"One minute he [was in front?]
of us, the next minute he was gone.
It's like he's a ghost or something."

"He's not a ghost," the third voice said, scoffing. "He plays the piano in a whorehouse, and whorehouse piano players don't just disappear. Keep your eyes open. He has to be down here somewhere."

Hawke moved slightly, and as he did so, he dislodged a brick which fell loudly against a stone.

"There he is!" one of them yelled, pointing toward Hawke. "Shoot him! Shoot the son of a bitch!"

All hell broke loose then. Guns roared and bullets screamed by, striking the bricks and stones. Flashes of orange light exploded around him.

Hawke was well positioned to pick out his targets. The three shooters were all in the open under the street lamp. They made perfect targets, and Hawke picked one of them off with one shot.

"He's got a gun!" one of the two remaining shooters yelled out.

Hawke hoped they would leave, now that they knew he wasn't an easy target. But they didn't leave.

"Kill him!" one yelled. "Kill him before he kills us."

Hawke shot two more times, and the final two went down.

The entire battle had taken less than a minute.

Books by Robert Vaughan

HAWKE
VENDETTA TRAIL
SHOWDOWN AT DEAD END CANYON
RIDE WITH THE DEVIL

ROBERT VAUGHAN

HAWKE
VENDETTA
TRAIL

HarperTorch
An Imprint of HarperCollinsPublishers

This is a work of fiction. Names, characters, places, and incidents are products of the author's imagination or are used fictitiously and are not to be construed as real. Any resemblance to actual events, locales, organizations, or persons, living or dead, is entirely coincidental.

HARPERTORCH
An Imprint of HarperCollins*Publishers*
10 East 53rd Street
New York, New York 10022-5299

Copyright © 2005 by Robert Vaughan
ISBN-13: 978-0-06-072586-0
ISBN-10: 0-06-072586-9

1-21-06 $ °°

First HarperTorch paperback printing: November 2005

HarperCollins®, HarperTorch™, and ❦™ are trademarks of Harper-Collins Publishers Inc.

Printed in the United States of America

Visit HarperTorch on the World Wide Web at www.harpercollins.com

10 9 8 7 6 5 4 3 2 1

This book is dedicated to my editor, Michael Shohl

HAWKE
VENDETTA
TRAIL

Chapter 1

WHEN MASON HAWKE RETURNED FROM THE CIVIL War he found, like many of his fellow Civil War veterans, that there was nothing left for him at home. So Hawke became a wandering minstrel, playing the piano in saloons and bawdy houses throughout the West. What practically no one who heard him playing "Cowboy Joe," or "Buffalo Gals" realized was that he was one of the most accomplished pianists in the world, having once played before the crowned heads of Europe.

That was a whole world and half a lifetime behind him, and Hawke never looked back in regret, never thought of what might have been. Instead, he continued to wander, knowing that somewhere on the other side of the next range of hills, or just beyond the horizon, there would be another town, another saloon, and another piano.

A seamstress in Texas thought he might be looking for love and she made herself available, but it didn't work out. A circuit-riding preacher told him he was looking for his soul . . . and Hawke agreed; at least in so much as he knew that his was a lost soul, but he had not yet found it.

Hawke did not openly seek trouble, but neither would he back away from it, and hotheaded hooligans would sometimes mistake the piano player for an easy mark. He had been pushed into more than one gunfight, and if truth were known, his adversaries did not always have to push that hard to get him to respond. When pushed into a fight, more often than not, someone would die. And then it would be time for Hawke to move on again.

It was that wanderlust that brought him to Nebraska City, Nebraska. He had just finished playing a set when the female proprietor of the saloon walked over to the piano carrying a mug of golden liquid, with a high, foaming head. She handed the beer to Hawke.

"Thanks, Callie," Hawke said. He blew away some of the foam, then took a drink.

Hawke was nearly six feet tall, clean shaven, with a square jaw and penetrating blue eyes. As always when he was working, he dressed well and at this moment was wearing a white ruffled shirt that was poked down into dark blue trousers. A fawn-colored jacket and crimson cravat completed his ensemble.

"Have you ever been to New Orleans, Mr. Hawke?" Big Callie Mouchette asked.

Big Callie got her nickname from her size. She was six feet tall and weighed three hundred and fifty pounds.

"No, I never have."

"You should go—someday. I'm from New Orleans, you know. You would love it there. In the theaters and opera houses you will find talented musicians playing beautiful music. And the food! Well, let's just say I didn't get to be this size by accident."

"You are a good, healthy-sized woman," Hawke said.

Big Callie laughed out loud, a robust, booming laughter that could be heard throughout the saloon.

" 'Healthy-sized'?" she said. She put her arms around Hawke's head and pulled him in between her massive breasts. "You are delightful, Mr. Hawke. Absolutely delightful. It was a fortunate day for all of us when you brought your charm and talent to Nebraska City. Now, play something for me. I'm going to sit right over there at that table and listen."

Hawke began playing "Lorena," a plaintive melody.

Hawke had been playing the piano at the Trail's End saloon in Nebraska City for two months now. Two months was an exceptionally long time for him to stay in one place and he was thinking about moving on, but the piano here was considerably better than the pianos he had played at most of the other watering holes he had worked.

And Big Callie Mouchette was an easy woman to work for. She was good-natured and generous with her employees. She also enjoyed classical music and often let Hawke play the kind of music he liked to play. Hawke appreciated that so much that he had already stayed much longer than he ever intended.

Another thing that kept Hawke here was that his time in Nebraska City had been very peaceful. But that all came to an end when his song was interrupted by a loud shout, followed by the crashing sound of a breaking bottle.

"You cheating son of a bitch!" a man shouted angrily.

Looking toward the disturbance, Hawke saw a man standing over a table, holding a broken whiskey bottle. Across the table from him was another man, sitting in a chair. There were streaks of blood on the sitting man's face, streaming down from a wound on his scalp. The two other players in the game had backed away from the table so quickly that their own chairs were on the floor, having been knocked over by their rapid withdrawal.

"By God, nobody cheats me and gets away with it," the man holding the bottle said.

"He wasn't cheating, you, Ford," one of the other players said.

"The hell he wasn't. I ain't won a hand in the last hour." Ford put the bottle down and reached for the money that was piled up in the middle of the table. "I'm just goin' to take this pot to make up for it."

"That's not your pot," the other player said.

Ford chuckled. "Well now, by God, it's my pot if I say it's my pot."

Big Callie, who had been sitting at her table listening to Hawke play, got up now and hurried over to the site of the disturbance. She began to treat the wounded man.

"Are you all right, Gary?" she asked, solicitously.

"Yes, ma'am," Gary answered groggily. "I'm a little woozy is all."

"If I catch you cheating again, you'll be more than a little woozy. You'll be a little dead," Ford said contemptuously as he started to put the money in his hat.

"Billy, did Mr. Fargo win that pot?" Big Callie asked one of the other players. She wet her silk handkerchief with whiskey and used it to treat Gary's wound.

"No, ma'm, he didn't. That's Gary's pot," Billy said. "You can ask Jimmy, he was in the game too."

"Billy's right," Jimmy said. "That ain't Ford's."

"Mr. Fargo, I think you'd better leave now," Big Callie said. "And leave the money on the table."

"The hell I will," Ford Fargo said. "I'm leavin', all right, but I'm takin' this money with me."

"I wasn't sitting at the card table," Big Callie said. "But there are three men who were, and all three say that this isn't your pot. If you take that money you will be stealing. And I don't condone stealing in my establishment."

"Come on, Big Callie, the son of a bitch was cheating," Ford said, pleading his case.

"He wasn't cheating you, Ford," Jimmy said. "He beat you fair and square."

"Now you're all taking up for him."

"We were in the same game as you. You think we would take up for him if he was cheating? Hell, we lost money too."

"Yeah, well, neither one of you lost as much money as I did."

"Neither one of them are as bad at cards as you are," Gary said. "You are an incredibly bad player, drawing two inside straights, running bluffs in games of stud when the cards clearly show that you don't have anything."

"Leave the money on the table, Mr. Fargo," Big Callie said again. She reached for Ford's hat and he jerked it away from her, then pushed her back away from him, pushing her so hard that the big woman fell to the floor.

Ford moved to stand over her and, pointing down at her, he snarled. "Stay out of things that don't concern you," he said.

Hawke had remained sitting at his piano bench, watching almost passively. He told himself it was none of his business, and he had no intention of getting involved until he saw Ford push Big Callie to the floor.

Then, sighing in resignation, Hawke stood up and walked over toward Ford. Ford either didn't see Hawke's approach or he saw him, but took no notice of him. That was no direct insult to Hawke, he was used to that. Piano players tended to fade into the background at saloons, becoming as invisible as a coatrack or a brass spittoon.

"Like I said, I'm takin' this money, unless there is someone in here who thinks he can stop me," Ford said as he returned to the table and continued filling his hat.

"That would be me," Hawke said.

"What?" Ford asked, looking at Hawke for the first time.

"You said unless there is someone who can stop you, and I'm saying that would be me. Put the money back on the table."

"What are you going to if I don't put the money back? Play a song for me?" Ford laughed at his own joke, and a few in the room laughed, nervously, with him.

"No. If you don't put the money back, I'll kill you," Hawke said easily.

Hawke's calm, almost expressionless reply surprised Ford, and the smile left his face.

Putting his hat full of money down on the card table, Ford raised his arm and pointed his finger at Hawke. "My advice to you, mister, is to go back over there to your piano and mind your own business."

A cold, humorless smile spread across Hawke's face. "You have just made your first mistake," he said in quiet, measured words.

"Oh yeah? And what would that be?"

"You are pointing your gun hand at me, but you aren't holding your gun."

"Don't you worry about my gun, you dandified son of a bitch," Ford said confidently. "I can get to it fast enough if I need to." He started to drop his arm.

The smile left Hawke's face. "No, leave your hand where it is."

"What?"

"Leave your arm pointing toward me," Ford said. "If I see it so much as twitch, I'll blow your head off."

Ford was caught between disbelief and fear. He was not used to anyone running a bluff on him, and he tried to laugh, though the laughter came out strained.

"What are you talking about? You don't even have a gun in your hand. Mister, you are crazy if you think I'm going to hold my arm out here like . . ."

Ford started to drop his arm but, in a lightning draw, Hawke had his pistol in his hand. The black hole at the business end of the barrel loomed large in Ford's face.

"No! Wait!" Ford shouted. He put both arms up.

For the moment the loudest sound to be heard was the steady ticktock of the Regulator clock that hung just above the fireplace mantle. The customers were as shocked as Ford by the Mason Hawke they were seeing now. They had come to know him only as a gentlemanly mannered, well dressed, and very talented piano player. They had never seen this side of him, and he could not have shocked them more if he had suddenly grown horns and a tail.

They observed the unfolding scene from their vantage points within the room, as intent on the proceedings as if they were the audience for a theatrical. In a sense, they were spectators in a theater, but in this case the scene being played out before them was much more intense than anything they had ever seen upon the stage. This was a drama of life or death.

Unable to control the sudden twitch that started in his left eye, Ford examined every face in the room, hoping to see someone he could count on for help. But he had run roughshod over the town for too long, using the town's fear of him as his weapon. He had no friends, and nobody offered to intercede for him.

Finally Ford looked back at Hawke, realizing that he was on his own.

"Please, mister," he said with a whimper. "What are you going to do?"

"Yes, Mr. Hawke, what *are* you going to do?" Big Callie asked, having been helped back to her feet now by Jimmy and Billy.

"I think I'll just shoot him," Hawke said easily.

"No! My God! Please! No!" Ford screamed.

"I'll leave it up to you, Miss Callie," Ford said calmly. "Do you want me to kill him? Or should I let him live?"

"I'm tempted to tell you to go ahead and shoot him," Big Callie said.

Ford began shaking uncontrollably, and he wet his pants. "Miss Callie, please don't let him kill me," he begged.

Big Callie sighed. "Go home, Mr. Fargo," she finally said in a contemptuous tone. "And don't come back here until you have learned to conduct yourself as a gentleman."

"Y . . . yes, ma'am," Ford stammered. He reached for his hat, then, pointedly, turned it upside down, dumping all the money back onto the table. Putting his hat back on, he turned to leave.

"Wait a minute," Hawke called.

Ford stopped.

"Before you leave, shuck out of that gun belt. The pistol stays here," Hawke said.

"The hell it does!" Ford said in one last attempt at bravado.

"Leave it," Hawke said coldly.

"Mister, I don't give my gun up to nobody. Nobody, do you understand that?"

Hawke pulled the hammer back on his pistol, and the deadly, metallic *click* sounded loud in the room. "I said leave it."

Ford paused for a moment longer, then, with shaking hands, unbuckled his gun belt. He let it drop to the floor.

"Now you can go," Hawke said.

"When do I get it back?" he asked.

"You don't get it back," Big Callie said.

"Are you crazy? There is no way I'm just going to give my gun to you."

"I won't give it back to you," Big Callie said "But if you send your papa in tomorrow, I'll give it to him."

"My pa? Do you really think I am going to send my pa in here?"

"If you want your gun back, you will," Big Callie replied.

Ford glareed at Big Callie and Hawke. The expression on his face was one of seething rage. "I'm going to remember this," he said. Pointedly, he looked at all the others in the room. "I'm going to remember you too," said, jabbing his finger toward them. "I'm going to remember every damn one of you."

As soon as Ford stepped through the door, a cheer went up in the saloon.

Hawke reached down to pick up the gun and belt that Ford had shed. Carrying it over to the bar, he handed it to the bartender.

"Here you go, Mike. Maybe you'd better keep this under the bar until his father comes for it."

"Yes, sir, Mr. Hawke," the bartender replied with a broad smile.

"Pour Mr. Hawke a drink, Mike," Big Callie said. "I think he's earned it, don't you?"

"Yes, ma'am, I'd say that he truly has," Mike said, reaching for the bourbon.

"Nobody takes my gun! Nobody!" Ford's loud, shrill voice shouted from just inside the door.

"Look out, he's got a shotgun!" one of the saloon patrons warned.

Hawke turned toward the door just in time to see the enormous muzzle flash of a double-barreled Greener.

Big Callie took the full load, grunting in pain and surprise as the buckshot opened up her chest. Blood sprayed from her like a fountain, and her corpulent body was slammed back against the bar. She slid down to the floor.

Ford pulled the trigger on the second barrel, but even as he did so, Hawke was firing at him. Ford's second load smashed into the piano at the back of the room.

Hawke fired only once, but his bullet caught Ford between the eyes and the young gunman pitched backward, falling through the swinging doors before crashing onto the board-walk out front. The smoke of three gun discharges hung in the air, the acrid bite burning the nostrils of the shocked spectators. The strings of the piano continued to hum in resonant vibration.

"Big Callie?" Gary said, getting up quickly from the floor where he had dived at Ford's opening barrage. He hurried over to examine her. "Oh, my God, Big Callie's been shot!"

Hawke stood for a moment longer with the smoking gun in his hand, then he dropped down on one knee to look at Big Callie. Putting his hand on her neck, he felt for a pulse but knew, even as he was doing so, that it was a waste of time. She was dead. He didn't have to tell anyone—everyone knew—and they moved toward her to look down in shocked silence.

Ford's body lay sprawled and unlamented on his back on the boardwalk in front of the saloon.

"What do we do now?" Billy asked.

"Somebody should get the sheriff, I reckon," Jimmy replied.

"What do we need him for? The one that killed her is already dead."

"Yes, but the sheriff needs to be told, don't you think?"

"Mr. Hawke, I expect you'd better get on out of town now," Mike said quietly.

"This was self-defense. I'll face the sheriff, even the court if I have to," Hawke said.

Mike shook his head. "No, sir, you don't want to do that. Not in this county. Ford's pa is Asa Fargo. He's the biggest rancher in the county, and even with everyone in here testifying that it was self-defense, I wouldn't feel all that good about your chances in a court of law."

Hawke looked toward the piano and saw a large, gaping hole in the soundboard cover. Several strings had been cut in two by the shot and were now protruding through the hole.

"Yeah, I guess you're right," Hawke said. He ran his hand through his hair. "Doesn't look there's much to keep me here now anyway."

It didn't take Hawke long to leave, once he made up his mind. It was his habit to travel light, carrying just what he could get in his saddlebags. He was saddled and out of town within a few minutes.

What nobody in the town realized, though, was that Hawke stopped just outside of town and camped on a hill that overlooked the cemetery. It might not be safe for him to attend Big Callie's funeral, but he intended to stay around until he saw her buried.

The next day dawned with a threat of rain that had still not been realized by midmorning when a small handful of people arrived at the cemetery. Hawke recognized a couple of them, and knew them to be cowboys who worked on the Fargo Ranch.

Although they made no demonstration of anger, or even sorrow over Ford's death, they did stand by respectfully as Ford's coffin was lowered into the ground.

Ford's father stood alone over the grave for a long moment. Hawke saw the sheriff ride up, dismount, and walk over to talk to him.

Hawke was too far away to hear what the sheriff was saying, but from the intense way they were talking, he got the idea that the sheriff might have been telling him the truth about what happened.

The sheriff ended his conversation by putting his hand on Fargo's shoulder. Fargo pinched the bridge of his nose, then nodded. Even though he had not been able to hear what was going on, Hawke realized at that moment that Fargo had accepted the sheriff's explanation and would not be coming after him.

Hawke was glad. He wasn't frightened of the old man. He just didn't want to kill him.

Not long after Ford Fargo was buried, Big Callie's funeral cortege arrived. Unlike the few who had come to watch Ford be put in the ground, nearly the entire town turned out for Big Callie's burial.

Hawke was too far away to hear the preacher, though every now and then a word or phrase would come up to him.

"Good woman. Friend to all. Lady of New Orleans."

The rain clouds delivered on their threat before the funeral was over and the rain sent many scurrying back to shelter. Finally the only people left were the two gravediggers who were closing Big Callie's grave. Hawke put on his slicker and stood under the tree, watching, until the last shovel of dirt had closed the grave.

Then, swinging into the saddle, he started riding southeast.

"All right, Miss Callie," he said aloud. "I think I'll just take a look at this New Orleans of yours."

Chapter 2

BECAUSE HE WAS IN NO PARTICULAR HURRY, MASON Hawke was taking the time to enjoy the beauty of the gentle Ozark Mountains. He rode alongside a wild and rushing stream whose surface frothed white when tumbling over the rocks, but was clear and silver when running free. As he rode, the path began to climb, and he crossed another creek, then mounted a wide, flat ridge. Cardinals and bluebirds flitted among the dogwood trees, while monarch butterflies floated just above a field of daisies. The hills were dappled green and brown in close, blue and purple as they marched off into the distance. Here and there a large jut of rock would lift itself from the verdant growth around it, showing the remains of the cataclysmic fault that had created the Ozark range at the dawn of the ages.

When Hawke made camp that evening, a squirrel came out onto a fallen log, chattering noisily as it scampered about trying to find and unearth some long-ago buried nugget. Hawke watched the squirrel for a few minutes, then he shot it.

"Sorry, squirrel," he said. "But I'm getting tired of beans without meat."

He skinned, cleaned, and then spitted the game, cooking it over an open fire. He watched the meat brown as his stomach growled with hunger. The squirrel was barely cooked before he took it off the skewer and began eating it ravenously, not even waiting for it to cool. When it was gone he broke open the bones and sucked out the marrow.

After his meal, he took inventory of his cheroots, counted four of them, cut each of them in half, then enjoyed a smoke. When his smoke was finished he let the song of a whippoor-will put him to sleep.

At dawn the next day the notches of the eastern hills were touched with the dove-gray of early morning. Shortly there-after, the rising sun spread a golden fire over the mountain-tops, then filled the sky with light and color, waking all the creatures below.

Hawke rolled out of his blanket and began digging through his saddlebag for coffee, but found none. Without coffee he had to make do with a tea made from boiled sassafras roots and sweetened with wild honey. He would have enjoyed a biscuit with his tea, but he had no flour. He had very few beans left and was nearly out of salt. The bacon had been used up a long time ago.

He took out half a cheroot, then lit it with a burning stick from the fire. After that he found a mossy rock protruding from the side of a hollow and went over to sit down and con-template his next move.

It was clear that he was going to have to go into town to re-plenish his supplies. The question was: Did he have enough money to do so or was he going to have to take a job for a while?

He emptied his billfold and turned his pocket out onto the rock. He counted six dollars, clearly not enough to last him all the way to New Orleans. He was going to have to find work somewhere, playing the piano if possible, though he had let his funds get so low that he would be willing to take a somewhat more physical job if it became necessary.

Four days later he came across a railroad and began following it south.

Toward midday he heard the high, keening sound of a steam-powered saw and knew that he was close to a town. As he came closer, he smelled meat cooking and bread baking. His stomach churned as those aromas reminded him of just how hungry he really was.

Finally he saw a church steeple rising through the trees, a tall spire, topped by a brass-plated cross that glistened in the high-noon sun. When he reached a road that was running parallel to the railroad tracks, he moved onto it and followed it the rest of the way into the settlement.

The town impressed him with its bustling activity. In addition to the working sawmill, there were several other examples of commerce: freight wagons lumbering down the street, carpenters erecting a new building, and a white apron-wearing store clerk who was sweeping the boardwalk in front of his place of employment.

Well-maintained boardwalks ran the length of the town on either side of the street. At the end of each block, planks were laid across the road to allow pedestrians to cross to the other side without having to walk in the dirt or mud. Hawke stopped his horse and waited patiently at one of the intersections while he watched a woman cross on a plank, holding her skirt up above her ankles, daintily, to keep the hem from soiling. She nodded her appreciation to him as she stepped up onto the boardwalk on the opposite side of the street.

When the woman had successfully negotiated the street, Hawke clucked at his horse, and it stepped across the plank, then headed toward the livery, a little farther down.

A lively game of horseshoes was in effect in an open lot

alongside the livery, and one of the players threw a ringer, evidenced by the clanging sound of the horseshoe hanging onto the stob. The ringer was followed by an equal round of cheers and groans.

Hawke dismounted in front of the livery stable.

A boy, no older than fourteen, came toward him.

"Take your horse, mister?" the boy asked.

"Yes, thanks," Hawke said as he removed his saddlebags, then snaked the Winchester out of its sheath. "Take his saddle off and give him a rubdown," he added, flipping a nickel toward the boy.

"Yes, sir!" the boy replied with a big smile, catching the nickel in midair.

An old man got up from the barrel he had been sitting on and walked, with a limp, over to Hawke. "How long will you be stayin'?" he asked.

"I'm not sure," Hawke said.

"It'll cost you fifteen cents a night," he said, nodding toward the horse. He pulled out a red handkerchief, blew his nose, then stuffed the handkerchief back into his pocket. "Or you can stay for a whole week for seventy-five cents. You save money that way."

"I don't know how long I'll be staying," Hawke said. "So we'll take it one night at a time. Does the fifteen cents include feeding him?"

"Hay, only. Oats'll cost you five cents extra."

Hawke gave him a silver dollar. "Give me eighty cents back and give 'im oats tonight. He's been ridden pretty hard for the last several weeks," Hawke said. "If I need to leave him in tomorrow, I'll be back."

"If you ain't paid for another night by four o'clock tomorrow afternoon, he'll be turned out," the old man warned.

"Sounds fair to me," Hawke said.

The old man gave him his change.

"By the way, where am I?" Hawke asked.

"Brown's Livery."

"No, I mean what is this town?"

"This here is West Plains, Missouri," the man said.

"Thanks. Seems like a nice, industrious town."

"We like it."

Suddenly several gunshots interrupted their conversation, and though they began echoing back from the surrounding hills, Hawke was able to discern where the initial shots came from. He looked quickly toward the opposite end of the street, where he saw two men backing out of a building. A sign, protruding over the boardwalk from the front of the building, identified it as the Bank of West Plains.

The two men were shooting back into the bank, whether at specific targets or just to provide cover for themselves, Hawke didn't know.

"Bank robbery!" someone called. "They're holdin' up the bank!"

The town-crier-like announcement wasn't really needed. Everyone on the street, from the sweeping store clerk, to the men loading a freight wagon, to those playing horseshoes, knew what was going on.

"Get the hell out of the way! Get off the street if you don't want to get shot!" one of the bank robbers shouted loudly, and he punctuated his shout by firing a couple of shots down the street. The shots had the effect he wanted, because everyone scattered.

A third man suddenly appeared from the alley that ran between the bank and the neighboring apothecary. He was riding one horse and leading two others. Leaning down, he handed the reins to the two bank robbers and, quickly, they climbed into the saddles. Mounted now, they started shooting up the town in order to keep people off the street.

Most of the townspeople had cleared out of the way, but

looking across the street, Hawke saw the woman who had crossed on the planking in front of him a moment earlier. She was still exposed, standing on the boardwalk in front of the millinery, absolutely frozen in fear.

"That woman needs to get out of the way," Hawke said.

"Oh my God, that's Emma!" the old man at the livery shouted. He pointed at the young woman. "That's my daughter!"

The window of the millinery shop shattered as a bullet hit it. Great shards of glass came crashing down onto the boardwalk around her. She let out a scream of fear, but was still too frightened to move.

Dropping his saddlebags, but holding on to his rifle, Hawke ran out into the street toward the woman, shouting at her as he did so.

"Go inside, miss!" he shouted. He was waving with his hand, indicating she should leave. "Go inside and get down!"

Hawke's immediate goal was to get the woman to safety, but by his action he had put himself in the path of the robbers' escape route. That made him a target and he heard a bullet whiz by his ear.

A second bullet kicked up dirt in the street very near him.

Turning toward the bank robbers, Hawke saw all three of them bearing down on him. Muzzle flashes and puffs of smoke from their pistols showed that all three were firing right at him, an indication underscored by the bullets that buzzed by his head like an angry swarm of bees.

Raising his Winchester to his shoulder, Hawke jacked a shell into the chamber, aimed at the one in the middle, and fired. Those who were watching from various vantage points around town saw a puff of dust and a mist of blood fly up from the impact of the bullet. Then, even as that robber was tumbling from his saddle, Hawke snapped the lever down and back up and fired a second time. A second robber fell as well, but this one didn't fall as cleanly as the first, because his foot got hung up in the stirrup and he was being dragged through the dirt.

Like a toreador avoiding the charge of a bull, Hawke stepped adroitly aside as the two horses pounded by: one empty and the other dragging its rider, who was now screaming at his mount to stop.

The third robber, as if just now realizing that he was alone, reined in his own horse, tossed his gun down, and threw both arms into the air.

"No, no!" he shouted. "Don't shoot, don't shoot! I quit, I quit!"

With the third bank robber's surrender, nearly a dozen armed men of the town came running out into the street with their guns aimed at the one remaining robber.

"Get down from there, mister," one of the men shouted in an authoritative voice. His authority, Hawke saw, came from the badge he was wearing on his vest.

Hawke hurried over to the woman.

"Miss, are you all right?" he asked. "Were you hit?"

"No, I'm . . . I'm fine," she answered in a weak and trembling voice.

The man at the livery was the first on the scene, arriving almost immediately after Hawke. He put his arms around his daughter and pulled her to him.

The next person on the scene was one of the horseshoe players. "Mister . . . that's about the bravest thing I ever seen," the horseshoe player said to Hawke. "I mean, the way you stood out there in the middle of the street and faced them three fellas down like that."

"I really didn't have much choice," Hawke replied. "I suddenly found myself trapped out in the middle of the street with nowhere else to go."

"The only reason you was trapped there was because you

was comin' over here to save my daughter," the liveryman said. He stuck his hand in his pocket and took out the silver dollar Hawke had just given him. "Here, take your money back. It's no good with me. Your horse can stay as long as he wants. And he'll be eatin' oats too."

"I appreciate that," Hawke said as he reached into his pocket to pull out the change the liveryman had given him. "No, sir, you can keep that too," the liveryman said.

Many of the other townspeople began arriving then, and they congregated on the boardwalk in front of the millinery shop.

"How's your daughter, Fred?" one of them asked.

"She's fine, thanks to this man," Fred said, indicating Hawke.

"Yeah, I seen him standing out there in the middle of the road, firin' that rifle like he was wielding Gideon's sword or somethin'," the local said.

The man Hawke had seen wearing the badge stepped up to speak to Hawke. He stuck out his hand. "I'm Sheriff Peach," he said. "And, mister, I want to thank you for what you done. You not only saved Miss Brown, you probably saved several others by stoppin' those men before they could shoot up the whole town. Not only that, you got the bank's money back. The whole town owes you for that."

Two men came up from the far end of the street then, bringing back the robber who had been dragged off by his horse. The robber was walking between them, unsteadily, but obviously not seriously wounded. There was a bullet hole in his shoulder, as evidenced by the black hole and stain of blood on his shirt sleeve.

"Sheriff Peach," one of the two men who was with the wounded prisoner called. "This here fella has been shot. You want we should put him in jail or take him down to see the doc?"

"Put the son of a bitch in jail," Sheriff Peach snarled.

"Wait a minute, I been shot," the robber complained. "You got to have a doctor look at me."

"Mister, I don't have to do anything but lock your sorry ass up," Sheriff Peach said. Then to the others he said, "Doc Allen's busy tendin' to the ones that was shot in the bank. He can look after this man when he's done with the others."

"How many got shot, Sheriff?" Fred asked. "And who was it?"

"There was two got shot. Joe Phillips and Leo Clark," Sheriff Peach replied. Clark is pretty bad gut shot. To tell the truth, I don't think he's goin' to make it."

"Oh, poor Mrs. Clark," Emma said. "She just had a new baby."

"If Clark dies, that means we're going to hang this-here fella," one of the two guards said. "So if you was to ask me, I don't know why Doc would want to even bother takin' the bullet out."

The prisoner, whose face was already contorted with pain, blanched.

"At least we're only goin' to have to hang two of the bastards," one of the other men said. He pointed toward the other man that Hawke had shot. "That one layin' out there is already dead."

Even as the man spoke, Hawke saw someone, dressed in a long black coat, standing out in the middle of the street, looking down at the body of the robber he had shot.

"Don't go plannin' nothin' fancy for that fella, Mr. Welch," one of the townspeople shouted. "We plan to put him away real cheap. As far as I'm concerned, you could just wrap him up in a tarp and bury him."

Some of the others around him laughed.

"The law says I have to put him in a box. But don't worry, Mr. Mayor. I will be very frugal," Welch called back.

Sheriff Peach looked back at Hawke. "What's your name, mister?"

"Hawke. Mason Hawke."

Mason Hawke waited for the inevitable reaction that his name caused. But, to his relief, the sheriff didn't seem to respond to it at all. Perhaps the town was too far off the beaten path for him to be recognized.

"Well, Mr. Hawke, I don't know what brought you to our town, but I'm sure glad you showed up when you did."

"I'm just passing through on my way to New Orleans," Hawke said.

"'Just passing through,' you say?" The sheriff chuckled. "Well, I reckon you will stay around long enough to collect your reward, won't you?"

"My reward?"

"I'd be willing to bet there's paper out on these fellas," Sheriff Peach said. "And even if there isn't, I'm pretty sure the town will want to come up with something. Wouldn't you say so, Mayor Felker?"

"Absolutely," Mayor Felker said.

"So what do you say? Are you going to stay around for the reward?"

Hawke smiled. "Oh, I think you can count on that," he replied.

"Mr. Hawke, have you had your lunch yet?" one of the town's citizens asked.

"No, I haven't."

"My name's Lambert. That's my café across the street there. You come on over and have lunch—on me."

"Thanks," Hawke said.

In addition to the lunch provided by Lambert's café, the town opened up the school auditorium that night for a potluck dinner. All the ladies of the town brought their special dishes, competing with each other for Hawke's attention.

Hawke was gracious to all of them, but one blackberry cobbler reminded him so much of the cobblers his mother used to make that he looked up the lady who brought it and gave her his personal thanks.

"Why, I'm just glad I could make it for you, young man," she said. "You doing so much for the town and all."

"What is your favorite song?"

"I beg your pardon?"

"I see a piano over there. If you will tell me your favorite song, I'll play it for you."

"You can play the piano?"

"Yes, ma'am."

"Oh, how wonderful. I think 'Home Sweet Home' would be my favorite. Do you know it?"

"Yes, ma'am, I do," Hawke said.

Hawke played the song for the lady who made the blackberry cobbler, then he took several more requests. That night he slept in the hotel, his room paid for by the bank.

As it turned out the three bank robbers were the Jensen Brothers. And as Sheriff Peach had suggested, they were wanted. The State of Missouri had put up a reward of one hundred dollars each for their capture. The next day the West Plains City Council voted to match the reward paid by the state, and they had a small ceremony during which they gave him the money.

"Did I hear you say you were going to New Orleans?" Fred Brown asked after the ceremony was over.

"Yes."

"On horseback?"

"That's what I had in mind."

Brown shook his head. "It'll take you another two weeks to get there by horseback. But you could board the train right here in West Plains and be there in two days."

"That's not a bad idea, but what would I do with my horse?"

"You can leave him with me, take him with you, or even sell him to me if you'd like. I'll give you twenty-five dollars for him."

"Make it fifty and I'll throw in the tack."

"Done," Brown said.

Chapter 3

HAWKE, WHO WAS SIX HUNDRED AND FIFTY DOL-
lars richer now than he had been when he arrived in West
Plains, stood in the predawn darkness, waiting for the south-
bound train. In the distance he heard the long mournful whistle of the approaching engine.

"Here she comes," someone said.

Shortly after the whistle, Hawke could hear the chugging
sound of the steam echoing through the hills, then, looking
down the track, he saw the huge gas lantern that was attached
just in front of the smokestack. The highly polished mirror
behind the lantern flame gathered and intensified the light to
cast a bright beam to illuminate the track ahead.

When the train arrived, Hawke could feel the power of the
engine as it pounded by. The whirling steel wheels were
nearly as tall as a man, turned by pumping driver rods that
were wreathed by the feathery wisps of steam that escaped
from the actuating cylinder. Still-burning embers dripped
from the firebox and lay glowing on the track beneath the
train.

The train squeaked and screeched as it drew to a stop in

front of the station. Even though it was at rest, it was still alive, venting steam from the relief valve like the gasps of some exhausted creature while its gearboxes popped and snapped as they cooled.

The conductor stepped down from one of the cars and looked out over the small assembly gathered. He pulled out his pocket watch, opened the cover, and examined it importantly. "How many do we have, John?" he asked.

"Three passengers, two express bags," the station master replied.

The conductor snapped the watch cover closed. "All aboard!" he shouted. Then to the station master, "Better get the express bags on quick. We're runnin' about half an hour behind."

"I'll get right on it," the station master promised, turning to hurry back to the depot.

Hawke waited politely until a man and his wife boarded, then he got on behind them. The interior of the car was lighted with gimbals-mounted lanterns and he walked down the aisle, passing passengers who were already aboard and sleeping through this stop, until he found an empty seat. Having bought a small suitcase to replace the saddlebags when he sold his tack to Fred Brown, Hawke now put the suitcase in the luggage netting just overhead. That done, he settled into his seat.

Almost immediately, it seemed, the train started forward in a series of halting, jerking motions until it began rolling smoothly. Shortly thereafter a porter came through the car extinguishing the lanterns. Hawke was sitting on the left side of the car and, through his window, he could see the first glimmering pink of dawn as the train headed south.

That evening Hawke changed trains in Memphis, Tennessee. Paying extra for a Pullman car, Hawke slept through the night, waking in Jackson, Mississippi, early the next morning. There, he changed trains again.

It was now early evening of the second day, and Hawke was in the dining car of the train he had boarded in Jackson. This train was known as *The City of New Orleans* and it was the last one he would have to board for this trip.

"Anything else I can get you, sir?" a white-jacketed steward asked, approaching Hawke's table.

Hawke, who had just enjoyed a dinner of roast prime rib of beef, brussels sprouts, and baked potato, picked up the napkin and dabbed at his lips.

"No, thank you. I'll just finish my coffee."

"Very good, sir."

"How long until we arrive in New Orleans?"

"I believe the conductor said we would be there in about an hour and a half," the steward answered.

"Thank you."

As Hawke sipped his coffee, he looked through the window that opened onto his table. Right now they were on a strip of land that separated Lake Pontchartrain from Lake Maurepas, and at this particular point it was so narrow that, from either side of the car he could see only water.

His coffee finished, he left the dining car and returned to his seat. Earlier in the afternoon the porter had given him a copy of the *New Orleans Picayune,* and Hawke decided to take advantage of the last light of the day to finish reading it.

He was startled to find a story about Big Callie in the newspaper.

CALLIE MARIE MOUCHETTE

Word has reached us by Western Union of the untimely passing of Mrs. Callie Marie Mouchette,

46, onetime resident of New Orleans. Living in Nebraska City, Nebraska, at the time of her demise, Mrs. Mouchette was proprietor of the Trail's End, a popular eating and drinking establishment in that city.

Many of our readers may recognize Mrs. Mouchette as the widow of Colonel Alphonso Mouchette, who died so gallantly in defense of the Honor of the South in the recent war.

He also found a story about the seamier side of New Orleans.

NEGROES MURDERED

Unrest at the city docks has become more widespread of late with the recent murder of two Negroes. It is believed that the Negroes were murdered by some of the gang of Sicilians who have become so lawless of late.

The Sicilians herein situated have formed gangs who, by their violence, extract tribute from their fellow countrymen, control nearly all the criminal elements of our fair city, as well as much of the normal activity of New Orleans' commerce.

There have been many complaints lodged about the Sicilian gangs, but the Mayor's office has all but admitted that the city is unable to handle the situation.

Police Commissioner David Hennesy believes the problem could better be laid upon the heads of the Negroes who, often, are placed in positions of authority and advantage over hard-working Whites.

That's an interesting take on the situation, Hawke thought as he finished the article. Placing the blame for the Negroes who were killed upon the very Negroes who were killed.

As the light had now grown too dim for further reading, he put the paper down. He watched the sun set over Lake Maurepas, setting the water afire with its dying color of blood red. A few minutes thereafter it grew totally dark and as Hawke continued to look through the window, he saw that they were coming into New Orleans.

The train passed by a very large estate with a beautifully manicured lawn and a huge house that reminded him of some of the palaces he had seen during his tour of Europe. He wondered who lived in such a house, and he watched it until he could no longer see it.

Chapter 4

~~~

IN A DARK ROOM OF THE SAME LARGE HOUSE
Hawke had observed, the gleaming orange burn at the end of
a cigar disclosed the fact that someone was standing at the
window, watching the train pass. Joseph Tangeleno, the man
with the cigar, was relatively tall for a Sicilian. Above his
powerful frame was an oversized head, furry eyebrows that
met in the middle, and deep-set, dark eyes. He continued to
watch the train until it disappeared around a distant curve in
the track.

Many suggested to Tangeleno that a man of his means
could afford to have a house farther away from the tracks, but
he always waved their suggestions aside. They didn't understand that he liked being this close to the railroad. He liked to
watch the trains when they passed by. The trains gave him a
visible link with a modern miracle which could, within a
matter of days, whisk someone from New Orleans to any
part of this huge country, from New York to San Francisco.

Joseph Tangeleno had been in America for twenty years,
but he still spoke with a heavy Italian accent. He was born in
Sicily, where membership in the Mafia was a way of life,

though the word "Mafia" was rarely used by its actual members. That is because "Mafia" is not an Italian word, and its definition has never been clearly established. Some say it means: "This honored thing of ours." The members called it la Cosa Nostra, the Arm, the Clique, the Outfit, the Tradition, the Office, the Honored Society, the Combination, or simply, the Family.

Back in Sicily, the Mafia adhered to a rigid code of the vendetta that took literally "an eye for an eye" and "a life for a life." It was this very code that brought Joseph Tangeleno to America in the first place. When Joseph's eighteen-year-old sister was dishonored, Joseph killed the man who was responsible. That forced him to come to America, not fleeing the law, but fleeing the family of the man he had killed.

Arriving in New Orleans, Tangeleno got a job at the riverfront, loading ships. Here, he found the same type of hierarchy he had dealt with in Sicily, only here, the man in charge was not Mafioso, or even a Sicilian. Here, the man in charge was a Cajun by the name of Henri Bejeaux.

Bejeaux controlled every aspect of life on the riverfront. Tangeleno had to get permission from Bejeaux to work, and he had to work the ships Bejeaux said he could work. He also had to pay Bejeaux a tribute, which Bejeaux called a "dock tax."

At first, it didn't bother Tangeleno all that much because he was used to living in hierarchical societies. But when he realized that Bejeaux wasn't being fair to him, or to any of the other Sicilians and Italians who lived and worked in New Orleans, he asked a couple of the other Sicilians who were being equally mistreated to go with him to have a talk with Bejeaux.

"What are you going to say to him, Tangeleno?" Nicholas Morello asked.

"I am going to ask him to listen to reason," Tangeleno replied.

"And if he will not listen to reason?" Sal Vizzini asked.

"I will let him know that I am disappointed."

Tangeleno, Morello, and Vizzini met with Bejeaux in his office. Taking onto himself the responsibility of speaking, not only for the three of them but for all the many Sicilians in New Orleans, Tangeleno presented their grievances. He told how the Sicilians were the last to get work, and when they did get work it was generally the most difficult jobs that paid the least. He further pointed out that the tributes the Sicilians had to pay were based upon a standard assessment and not by the job. That meant that while they were given the jobs that paid the least, they were assessed the same as the other workers.

"Is that it?" Bejeaux asked when they were finished. "What do you want me to do about it?"

"I thought you might listen to reason," Tangeleno said.

"Get out of my office, you guinea bastards," Bejeaux said with a dismissive wave of the back of his hand.

Tangeleno didn't say another word. Instead he stood, nodded at the other two, and they left. Tangeleno didn't go far. When he came to work that day he brought a shotgun with him, which he hid behind some loose boards in the closest warehouse. Now, in full view of the others, Tangeleno retrieved the shotgun, loaded both barrels, then went back into Bejeaux's office.

"What do you want now?" Bejeaux asked.

Tangeleno didn't answer him. Instead, he pulled both triggers on the shotgun and blew away half the Cajun's head.

Tangeleno "made his bones" on that day and was accepted, immediately, by the other Sicilians as a man of honor. Within a short time after that, he was occupying the same position Bejeaux had occupied: assigning jobs and accepting tributes from the other workers.

He soon saved enough money to buy the *Avanti*, a fast, 800-ton side-wheeler, which he put into the shipping business. Shortly thereafter, the Civil War began and Tangeleno used the *Avanti* as a Union blockade runner. That made Tangeleno a hero to the South, because the *Avanti* brought in much needed goods. But it also helped Tangeleno, because the goods that did make it through the blockade brought top dollar.

Tangeleno's loyalty to the South only extended so far, though. He would not accept payment in Confederate money. He demanded—and got—gold, silver, or federal dollars. Joseph Tangeleno was a very successful blockade runner and by the end of the war, he was an exceptionally wealthy man.

New Orleans was slow in recovering from the war. Although it had not been physically destroyed, as had Atlanta and some of the other Southern cities, it had been invaded by Carpetbaggers. Carpetbaggers were Northern opportunists who came into the city to take possession of all commercial, as well as political, vantage points.

In the minds of the residents of New Orleans, the police, the city hall, the state house, and the federal government were all entities that had been put in place by the reconstructionists to make Southern citizens suffer as their punishment for participating in the war. As a result, most of its citizens no longer thought in terms of U.S., state, or even local government for functions and services.

This was especially true among the immigrants of the city, and when a local businessman wished to establish a grocery store, a laundry, a bakery, or a restaurant, he didn't go to any government facility. When a woman wished to make arrangements to bring over her mother and father from the old country, she didn't go to Immigration. When seeking redress for a grievance, the injured party didn't go to the Justice Department.

In New Orleans, where one went, on all these occasions, was to Joseph Tangeleno. Tangeleno, they knew, had the connections and the resources to get things done. But he was not the only one they came to when they needed help against some transgression; he was also the one they feared when they were the transgressors. He was the final authority, the benevolent dictator, and when he was spoken to, it was always with a respectful "Don" before his name.

To outsiders, it might appear that Tangeleno was running a monolithic organization, but in fact, he now had an adversary, a much younger and very ambitious man named Carlos De Luca. De Luca was born in America, so he had the best of both worlds: American citizenship and very close ties with his Sicilian connection. De Luca called his organization the Family. His second in command—and enforcer—was Vinnie Provenzano.

Chapter 5

ON THE NEXT MORNING AFTER HAWKE ARRIVED in New Orleans, he came out of the hotel and stepped up to a hack that was parked at the curb.

"Do you know a place called House of the Evening Star?" he asked the driver.

The driver smiled. "Indeed I do, sir, I know it well," he said. "Oh, not that I ever go there, mind you, I'm married, you see. But from what I've heard, it is the finest whorehouse in all of New Orleans. You won't be disappointed. No, sir, I can guarantee you that."

"How?"

"I beg your pardon?"

"If you've never been there, how can you guarantee that I won't be disappointed?"

The driver laughed. "Well, sir, I guess you've got me on that one," he said. "I was just going by what all the gentlemen say."

"That sounds good enough to me," Hawke said as he climbed into the back of the hack. The driver snapped the reins and pulled away from the curb. The steel-rimmed wheels of the hack made a ringing sound against the brick-paved streets, accompanied by the staccato rhythm of the horse's hooves, while Hawke sat back to take in his first impressions of New Orleans. It took less than ten minutes to travel from the hotel to the House of the Evening Star.

The house was a large white two-story edifice surrounded by a ground-floor porch and an upstairs balcony. Both were decorated with iron scrollwork and dripped with wisteria. A brick walk approached the house under spreading magnolia trees, their large white blossoms shining brightly from the deep green waxy leaves.

"I know who you are, Mr. Hawke," Clarisse Grangier said a moment later, after she let Hawke into the house and he introduced himself. She dabbed at the tears in her eyes. "My sister wrote all about you."

"Callie was a wonderful woman," Hawke said.

"Thank you for coming to see me. I knew she was dead, of course. Her lawyer sent me word. But it was very sweet of you to come see me in person."

"It was the least I could do," Hawke said. "Besides, I wanted to have a look at this New Orleans she was always talking about."

"What are you going to do here? How long are you going to stay?"

"I'm not sure. I may try and find a job somewhere, but I probably won't stay for more than a month or two. If I stay in any one place for too long, I start getting irritable and out of sorts." Hawke ameliorated his comment with a wide smile.

"My sister said you were a wonderful pianist," Clarisse said. "And she called you a pianist, not a piano player."

"Callie would know the difference," Hawke said. "She had a wonderful appreciation for music."

"I don't have the same music appreciation she did, but I

do like pretty music. How would you like to play the piano for me?"

"Are you offering me a job?"

"Yes. You could play the piano for us here, at the House of the Evening Star. I think we are already one of the classiest places in New Orleans, but having a"—she paused, in order to set the word apart—"pianist . . . would make it even classier. What do you say, Mr. Hawke? Will you play for me?"

"All right, Miss Clarisse, I'll play for you," Hawke agreed. "As long as you understand that I'm not making any long-term commitments here."

"A day, a week, a month," Clarisse said. "We'll just enjoy your music while you are here."

As Hawke stood there talking to Clarisse, a well-dressed man came down the stairs.

"Hello, Mr. Vizzini," Clarisse said. "How nice of you to visit us today."

"Hrrmph." Vizzini growled.

"My, isn't he in a good mood?" Clarisse said with a chuckle.

A moment later a woman came down the stairs. When she saw Clarisse, she put her hand to her face, then turned away so she couldn't be seen clearly. She hurried down the rest of the stairs before disappearing in the kitchen.

"Evangeline?" Clarisse called. "Evangeline, are you all right?"

"I'm fine," Evangeline mumbled.

"You don't look fine. What are you hiding?"

"Nothing."

"Turn your face so I can see it."

Reluctantly, Evangeline turned toward Clarisse. When she did, Hawke saw that one of her eyes was black and swollen nearly shut. Her lip was puffed up.

"Good Lord, child! Did Vizzini do that to you?"

"He wasn't angry or anything," Evangeline said quickly. "He just got a little carried away, that's all."

"'A little carried away'? It looks to me like he got a *lot* carried away."

"I'll be fine," Evangeline mumbed as she turned to go into the kitchen.

"Does that happen often?" Hawke asked.

"Not every time," Clarisse answered. "But, with Vizzini, it happens more times than it should. Evangeline is absolutely the only one who will have anything to do with him."

"Why does she have anything to do with him? Seems to me like the smartest thing to do would be to avoid him."

"Evangeline has the crazy idea that Vizzini is going to marry her."

"Where did she get that idea?"

"She says that he tells her he intends to marry her," Clarisse said. "But, of course, if he did say that, and I have no reason to doubt Evangeline's account of it, he is just playing with her. There is no way that a Sicilian is going to marry a Cajun."

"You should talk to her," Hawke suggested.

"Oh, believe me, I have talked to her many times," Clarisse said. "It does no good. But enough of this," she added with a broad smile. "When can you start?"

Hawke walked over to the piano, sat down, and smiled up at Clarisse. "If it's all right with you, I'll just start right now," he said.

He began playing "Claire de Lune."

Chapter 6

JOSEPH TANGELENO CALLED A MEETING OF ALL his lieutenants. De Luca had been getting more and more aggressive, and it was time to deal with the problem.

"Don Tangeleno, they are here," Nicholas Morello announced when all had arrived.

"Grazi."

Tangeleno followed Morello into the parlor, where half a dozen men were standing around, engaged in general conversation. All conversation halted as Tangeleno came into the room and the men turned toward him.

"Noi salutiamo lei con rispetto, Don Tangeleno," the men said as one.

Tangeleno acknowledged their respectful greeting with a nod of his head, then indicated that all should sit down.

"Let us begin the meeting," Tangeleno said. "Vizzini, how are things at the riverfront?"

"Things have improved with the Coloreds," Vizzini said. "Some of them had quit paying their labor dues and were declaring their loyalty to De Luca. We made an example of a couple of them, and many of the others have come back around."

"Are the police still investigating?" Tangeleno asked.

"No, Don Tangeleno," Vizzini answered. "In the first place, nobody really cares about a few dead Coloreds. Besides, some of the Coloreds that we can trust are spreading the rumor that the killing was actually a fight over women."

"How do you know we can trust them?"

"We are paying them," Vizzini said.

"Buono, buono," Tangeleno said, nodding appreciatively.

One by one, Tangeleno's other lieutenants gave their reports on such things as: gambling, protection, and the somewhat more legitimate operations, such as tribute from workers on their roster and city sewage and water. In every case, they reported some friction brought about by interference from the De Luca Family.

"Don Tangeleno, something is going to have to be done about De Luca," Morello said. "He is attempting to take more than his share of water from the well."

Tangeleno nodded. "I agree. Morello, I am going to call on your services."

"Io sono il sou ser luigire, don Tangeleno," Morello said with a slight bow. "I am your servant," he repeated in English.

"You will not fail me?"

"Io non falliro."

"Buono, buono, because I would be very disappointed if you failed me."

"What would you have me do, Don Tangeleno?"

"I want you to go to Carlos De Luca and to Vinnie Provenzano. Offer them both my personal greetings and my personal best wishes. Set up a meeting between us."

"Sí, Don Tangeleno," Morello said.

* * *

Hawke had not been in New Orleans very long before he had his first encounter with one of New Orleans's many Sicilian immigrants. The run-in did not happen in the House of the Evening Star, but occurred at a grocery store in the neighborhood.

The store was just a few buildings down the street from the Evening Star. There were three little girls skipping rope in front of the building next to the grocery store and Hawke smiled and waved at them as he pushed open the door to go into the store. A little bell rang as the door was opened.

The store was typical of the neighborhood grocery stores and it smelled of flour and smoked meats and sorghum molasses. A gray-haired, pleasant-looking man came toward him. The man was wearing a white apron.

"Yes, sir, may I help you?"

"You are Mr. Garneau?"

"Yes."

"My name is Mason Hawke, Mr. Garneau. I'm working for Clarisse Grangier."

Garneau looked surprised. "You are working for Miss LeGrand?"

Hawke chuckled. "I play the piano for her," he said.

Garneau laughed as well, then nodded. "Ah, yes, that I can understand."

"I have an introductory note from Miss Grangier and a shopping list for some items she wants charged to her account."

Garneau waved his hand. "I don't need the note from Miss Grangier. Just give me the shopping list," he said. "Your word is good enough for me."

Hawke handed the grocer his list and the grocer started filling it, going to various shelves and bringing the items back to put on the counter. Hawke wandered to the back of

the store and started looking around. Then he suddenly saw
Garneau run out the front door.

"Get out of here!" Garneau shouted. "Get out of my
store!"

The shout was followed by the sound of two gunshots, then
the crashing of a window. Hawke had his pistol in his hand
instantly, and he darted through the front door and onto the
sidewalk. He saw Garneau sitting on the ground in front of
the store, holding his hand over a bleeding wound.

Garneau was looking at the man who had shot him, not in
fear or anger, but almost in detachment, as if this were all
happening to someone else and he was just a bystander.

"Mr. Garneau!" Hawke shouted as he bent over to see to
him.

The gunman who had shot Garneau now fired at Hawke,
and Hawke heard the bullet whiz by and slam into the veg-
etable stand just beside him.

Hawke raised his gun to fire back, but saw the gunman
running toward the three little girls, the same little girls
Hawke had seen skipping rope, but now they were just standing there watching.

"No, stop!" Hawke shouted.

Hawke knew exactly what the gunman had in mind. He was
going to use one or more of the girls as his shield. If Hawke
was going to get a shot, he would have to take it right now.

Hawke pulled the trigger and the gun boomed and kicked
back in his hand. His bullet caught the gunman high in the
chest, knocking him down and causing him to drop his pistol.
Hawke ran toward the pistol as the gunman was trying to re-
trieve it. He managed to kick it away, right from under the
gunman's fingertips, then he pointed his pistol right at the
gunman's head.

"Lie still," he ordered.

"You shot me!" the gunman gasped. "I didn't think you'd take a chance with the little girls so close. Are you crazy?"

Hawke looked back toward the wounded grocer and saw that a couple of people were bent down over him.

"How is he?" Hawke asked.

"He needs a doctor, but I don't think the bullet hit any of his vitals," one of the two men replied.

"I need a doctor too," the gunman said.

Hawke put his pistol away and leaned down to look at the man's wound. The bullet had hit high in the shoulder and though the shock of its impact had knocked the gunman down, Hawke didn't believe it was a serious wound.

"You'll live," Hawke said.

"You made a big mistake by shooting me," the gunman said. "I'm part of the De Luca Family. I'm protected."

"De Luca Family? What are you talking about? Is there a family feud between the De Lucas and the Garneaus."

The gunman blinked. "I'll be damned. You don't know what I'm talking about, do you?"

"I know you shot Mr. Garneau and you shot at me," Hawke said.

"Mister, your days are numbered," the wounded gunman said.

Two policemen arrived then, brought to the scene by the sound of gunfire. Both policemen had their guns drawn.

"You!" one of them shouted at Hawke. "Put your hands up!"

"Not him!" Garneau said. "He came to help. It's the other one you want. His name is Rosario Meli."

"All right, step out of the way," the policeman said to Hawke.

Hawke did as they asked, then he stood by Garneau and watched as, not too gently, they jerked Meli to his feet. They put his wrists in shackles, then led him away.

"You knew him?" Hawke asked.

"Yes. He belongs to the De Luca Family."

"De Luca? I thought you said his name was Meli."

"His name is Meli, but he is Mafioso."

"Mafioso?"

"Many of the Sicilians have banded together in a society of criminals. It's as if they have their own army. You can't attack one of them without attacking them all."

"That seems pretty elaborate just to protect a thief."

"He wasn't stealing from me," Garneau said. "Not in the way you think. He was trying to sell me insurance. If you buy their insurance, they won't harm you or your store. If you don't buy it, they will harm you or your store. I've refused to buy their insurance, and Meli was here to teach me a lesson."

"I've never heard of such a thing."

"You'll hear more about it if you stay here long enough," Garneau said. "Especially now that you have made yourself their enemy."

"Make way! Make way!" Someone was shouting and, looking up the street, Hawke saw an ambulance approaching, pulled rapidly by two horses whose hooves were clattering loudly on the brick-paved street.

The next day a meeting took place in Todaro's restaurant, on the corner of Chartres and Ursulines streets. The three big dining rooms were crowded with tables, statues of the Madonna, splashing fountains, figures of birds, potted plants, oversized paintings, and hanging tapestries.

Todaro had not chosen the role of mediator between Tangeleno and De Luca. It had been thrust upon him by the popularity of his restaurant. His restaurant was a favorite spot due to the quality and the quantity of the food he served. As soon as a diner was seated, he would be brought a big hunk of cheese and a loaf of Italian bread, followed by artichokes and peppers. Steaming plates of pasta were served, followed by the entrée of veal parmigiana, or chicken cacciatore, or roast chicken, or filet of sole. After that came the deep-fried bugie, sugar-dipped and crunchy. And if one was still hungry, there was an entire assortment of pies, cakes, and ice creams.

Morello, who was Tangeleno's *secondo in commando*, met with Sal Provenzano, who was De Luca's second in command, to work out the details for the meeting. Todaro was informed of the meeting and agreed to set aside a room for them.

Once the participants were seated around the table, which had already been set to prevent any unwanted interruptions by waiters, the meeting would begin. It would last as long as necessary, without intrusion from Todaro or any of his waiters, unless something was specifically asked for.

"All right, Tangeleno, you asked for this meeting," De Luca said. "What's on your mind?"

De Luca specifically avoided use of the term "Don," thereby indicating that he considered himself at least equal to Tangeleno in rank and authority.

"To begin with, I would like to thank you for agreeing to this meeting," Tangeleno said.

De Luca nodded. The others around the table began to eat. This wasn't a demonstration of rudeness on their part, nor did it indicate a lack of interest in the proceedings. It was just the way of things. When such meetings were conducted over the dinner table, eating the food was an expression of the goodwill of the participants.

"I believe we are coming into a new time," Tangeleno said. "Many of our people have come to America from Sicily, and they have spread throughout the country. I now have connections in Memphis, St. Louis, Kansas City, Denver, and San Francisco. I will soon have a connection in New York. I can send a telegram and get a reply in the same day. I can board a train and be to any of these cities in just over one week. What a wonderful and marvelous time we live in. Everywhere we look we see that the old ways are behind us. Because of all this, it is time for some changes to be made . . . some very important changes."

"What kind of changes do you have in mind?" De Luca asked.

"I think we could organize a Family in every city, with each of those Families to have its own *capo*. Think of the power of our movement if we were organized in Memphis, St. Louis, Kansas City, Denver, San Francisco, and New York."

"That brings us to New Orleans," De Luca said.

"Yes."

"We are already organized in New Orleans."

"Yes, but we have two Families here, when we should only have one."

"And one *capo*?"

"Yes," Tangeleno answered. "With one *capo*."

"I see. And that would be you, I suppose?"

"No. That would be you."

De Luca blinked in surprise. He stared at Tangeleno for a long moment, then he studied the others around the table before coming back to Tangeleno.

"Wait a minute. What is this?" De Luca asked. "I can't see you merging your people with mine and making one Family with me at the head. You have something else in mind, don't you?"

"Yes," Tangeleno admitted. "I do have something else in mind." Tangeleno touched the napkin to his lips, then leaned back in his chair and pressed the tips of his fingers together, studying De Luca for a long moment before he answered. "I would propose myself as *capo di capi*."

"You want to make yourself the boss of bosses?"

"Yes." Tangeleno took a forkful of spaghetti. "Every Family will have a boss, but I will be the boss of bosses."

"Why should I agree to that?"

Tangeleno had to wait until he swallowed before he answered, then he held up his finger as if asking for a moment.

"I have been here much longer than you, Carlos. I keep a good set of books on every operation: the riverfront, the gamblers, the banking, all of it. I know how much money each enterprise brings in and I know how much money each enterprise costs to operate. I also know which police officers work which beats and how much it takes to keep them all quiet. I know which judges will turn their eyes aside and how much it costs to arrange that. Everything is going very smoothly—and that is not by accident. That is because I have been doing this for much longer than you.

"In fact, you might say that I am already *capo di capi*. If we are to organize in all those cities I just mentioned, it will be because they got their start from me."

"I didn't get my start from you," De Luca said, pointing to his chest with his thumb. "I started on my own. You say you will merge your Family with mine, but what you are really saying is that you want me to merge my Family with yours."

"Carlos, is it not true that one of your men, Rosario Meli, was recently shot when he tried to collect insurance from the grocer, Garneau?"

"Yes, this is true."

"What have you done about that?"

"I have done nothing yet, but . . ."

Tangeleno held up his hand to interrupt him. "To show you my sincerity, and as an act of good faith, I say to you now, do not worry about this man who shot Rosario Meli. For, even as we speak, I have sent some of my men to take care of him. That will discourage anyone else from interfering with any of our people."

De Luca let out a long sigh, then he drummed his fingers on the table for a moment or two. "Let me consider this offer you have made," he said.

"Consider it carefully, my friend," Tangeleno said. "It is a reasonable offer, and I hope you will listen to reason."

Chapter 7

HAWKE WENT TO THE THEATER TO HEAR THE NEW
Orleans Symphony Orchestra in concert. The orchestra was
directed by Professor Leonard Tompkins, and tonight the
music of Beethoven was featured.

Although Hawke knew Tompkins, he remained in the back
of the theater and made no effort to contact him. That was because Tompkins was from a part of Hawke's life that no
longer existed, and he believed it was best to leave it that way.

As Hawke walked home after the concert, he had the feeling that someone was following him. The House of the Evening Star was actually on Bourbon, between St. Ann and
Dumaine, but because he thought he was being followed, he
passed by both St. Ann and Dumaine and turned on St. Philip.

Whoever was behind him turned as well.

Hawke chose this route, not only to see if he actually was
being followed, but also because he knew there were several
open lots. One of the lots was filled with bricks and stone,
preparatory to some impending construction. If he was being
followed, this would be a good place to confront them.

When Hawke drew even with the lot, he stepped off the

street and slipped in behind a pile of quarried stone. Pulling his gun, he looked back into the direction from which he had come.

There were three of them, and they turned onto Dauphine, then paused for a moment under the flickering streetlamp.

The men began speaking, but as they were speaking in Italian, Hawke couldn't understand anything they were saying.

"What the hell?" one of them said. "Where did he go, Emilio?"

"I don't know, one minute he was right in front of us, the next minute he was gone," Emilio said. "It's like he's a ghost or something."

"A ghost," the third voice said, scoffing. "He's not a ghost. He plays the piano in a whorehouse and whorehouse piano players don't just disappear. Keep your eyes open. He has to be down here—somewhere."

Hawke moved slightly, and as he did so, he dislodged a brick, which fell rather loudly against a stone.

"There he is!" one of them yelled, pointing toward Hawke. This time he yelled the words in English, so Hawke knew that they were not only looking for him, they had found him.

"Shoot him! Shoot the son of a bitch!"

All hell broke loose then. Guns roared and bullets screamed by, striking the bricks and stones. Flashes of orange light exploded around him.

Hawke was well positioned to pick out his targets. The three shooters, on the other hand, were all in the open and bunched together under the streetlamp. They made perfect targets, and Hawke picked one of them off with one shot.

"He's got a gun!" one of the three shouted in panic.

Hawke hoped they would leave, now that they knew he wasn't an easy target. But they didn't leave.

"Kill him! Kill the son of a bitch before he kills us!" the other yelled.

His two attackers continued to shoot at him, and Hawke had no choice but to return fire.

Hawke shot two more times, and the final two went down.

Then it was quiet, except for the barking of some nearby dogs. A little cloud of gun smoke drifted up over the deadly battlefield and Hawke walked out among the fallen assailants, moving cautiously, his pistol at the ready.

The caution wasn't necessary. All three men were dead and the entire battle had taken less than a minute.

Putting his gun away, Hawke stepped back through the empty lot and out into the alley. He followed the alley across St. Philip and Dumaine, turning down St. Ann until he reached Bourbon Street. Then, even as he heard the police whistles a few blocks behind him, he reached the House of the Evening Star.

The parlor was nearly empty when he went in; most of the callers were upstairs with the girls. There was one man sitting on the sofa with Clarisse. Clarisse got up and walked over to meet him when Hawke came in.

"How was the concert?" she asked.

"It was very nice," Hawke replied. "I appreciate you allowing me the time off."

"Nonsense," Clarisse replied. "I figure every day you remain here is a bonus, and if I can keep you here a bit longer by giving you time off when you ask for it, I am more than willing to do what I can to make your time here happy."

"Are you entertaining customers now?" Hawke teased, nodding toward the man on the sofa.

"Yes, but only those with the most discriminating tastes," Clarisse said, laughing.

Hawke went over to the piano and sat down.

"You don't have to work tonight, Mason," Clarisse said.

"This isn't for work, this is for me," Hawke said as he began playing 'Bach's Fugue in G.'

* * *

The next day one of the girls who worked at the House of the Evening Star was preparing to go downstairs for the evening rush of business. Looking into the mirror, she used a small brush and a rouge pot to add a bit of color to her cheeks.

Rachel was quite pretty, with high cheekbones, full eyelashes, a small turned-up nose, and blonde ringlets that cascaded down either side of her face. Her broad smile showed even white teeth.

She had just about finished when there was a quiet knock on her door.

"Miz Rachel?" someone called. "Miz Rachel, you be in there?"

When Rachel opened the door, she was greeted by Doney, the black maid, who handed her a letter.

"This here letter just come and Miz Clarisse said give it to you."

"Thanks, Doney," Rachel said, taking the letter. "Is it getting crowded down there yet?"

"I ain't looked down there none, but I spec there's quite a few menfolks here already."

"I'd better get down there then. If anyone asks about me, tell them I'll be down directly."

"Yes'm, I do that," Doney said.

Rachel shut the door, then looked at the envelope. The letter was from Bellefont, Kansas, and she smiled. This would be a letter from Louise Smalley. Louise used to work here, until she got married.

Rachel debated whether she should read it now, or put it aside and go downstairs. The debate didn't last long, nor was the issue ever seriously in doubt. She sat at her dresser and opened the envelope.

Dear Rachel,

Your letter of the 5th at hand, I take pen to paper and answer in the hope that this finds you and all the other girls there a doing fine.

I know you and all the other girls thought I was crazy to marry someone I had never met before he come into the whorehouse that first time. But marrying Eddie Smalley is the best thing that ever happened to me.

All of Eddie's friends were really surprised when he returned from New Orleans with a wife, and now everyone wants to know how we met. Eddie tells them I was the preacher's daughter—and we met in church.

That works, because as you may remember, I really was a preacher's daughter before I went on the line. Of course my father died long before that happened, which is good, because I don't think I could have faced him if he knew what I became.

You know what they call whores here in Bellefonte? They call them soiled doves. Isn't that a nice name for them? The town is so small that there are only two, and I've met both of them.

I told one of them, Maggie, what I was and she has been very good about keeping it secret.

Rachel, there is a gambling house here called the Queen of Hearts. I have heard that it is for sale. If you have managed to save any money, I think this would be a very good buy for you. I think you would like it here. It's a lot different from New Orleans, but you would get a fresh start.

Your friend,
Louise

Rachel smiled at Louise's letter, then added it to the packet of letters she had already received from her. Louise was the only one Rachel ever got mail from, and she enjoyed the correspondence because her letters gave Rachel a glimpse of what the world was like beyond this house.

She thought about Louise's invitation to come out to Kansas and buy a gambling house. The idea was intriguing, but she had not been as frugal as she should have been, so she hadn't saved that much money. She was sure she didn't have enough money to buy it alone, but perhaps she and Fancy could buy it together. At least, it was something she could think about.

Putting the packet of letters in a little rosewood box that sat on her dresser, she took one last look at her reflection in the mirror, then left her room and went downstairs.

"Do you know any of these men?" the police captain asked Joseph Tangeleno. He pulled back a tarpaulin to reveal three men, all dead by gunshot.

Tangeleno nodded.

"Would you identify them, please?"

"That is Emilio Catalani," Tangeleno said, pointing to the first one. Then he pointed to the next two. "Domenico Spontini, Agostino Allegri."

"They belonged to your organization?"

"They were . . . employees," Tangeleno said without being specific. "They handled things for me down at the riverfront."

"Yes," the police captain said. "I know how they handle things for you. Do you have any idea who shot them? Or why?"

"No, I don't know who shot them," Tangeleno said. "Where did you find them?"

"We found them in an empty lot in the 1100 block of Dauphine."

Tangeleno looked up quickly. "The 1100 block of Dauphine?"

"Yes. Do you think it means anything that where they were found is not too far from Carlos De Luca's house?" the police captain asked.

"No," Tangeleno replied. "Do you think it means anything?"

"We've been getting rumors that there is bad blood between you and De Luca."

"I wouldn't say there is bad blood," Tangeleno said. "We are both Sicilian. Sometimes, like brothers, we will have a little disagreement."

"I would not like to see a war start in New Orleans," the police captain said.

Chapter 8

~~~

AN HOUR LATER, AT HIS HOME, TANGELENO WAS
meeting with his two top lieutenants, Morello and Vizzini.

"They were found near De Luca's house," Tangeleno said.
"He had to be the one who did it. Who else would kill three of
our men like that?"

"Emilio was pretty hotheaded," Morello said. "I'm sure he
made enemies down on the riverfront."

"Down on the riverfront? Nothing down there but Coloreds and Micks. Do you think a colored man or an Irishman
would dare to do anything like this? I'll answer that for you.
No, they wouldn't. De Luca is the only one who would, and
the only one who could kill all three of them like this."

"But why would he do that? You sent them after that piano
player as a gesture of goodwill," Morello said.

"That's exactly why he did it," Tangeleno replied. "He was
telling me that he didn't want my help, didn't want anything
to do with me. It was a slap in my face."

"So what do we do now?" Vizzini asked.

"We cannot let this go any further," Tangeleno said. "The

way I see it now, I have been challenged by De Luca. I have to answer him, and the only way to do that is to kill him."

"But, Don Tangeleno, if we kill him, would that not end any chance of ever consolidating our two Families?" Morello asked.

"Probably," Tangeleno admitted. "But the way I see it now, we have no other choice."

"Don Tangeleno, wait," Vizzini said.

"Wait? Wait for what?"

"I have an idea. Instead of killing De Luca now, why don't we just kill three of his men?"

"What good would that do?"

"If we kill three of his men, we can go to him on equal footing," Vizzini said. "He has killed three of ours, we have killed three of his. There would be no need for a vendetta. I think De Luca would understand then that it is better to live in peace than war."

"Perhaps," Tangeleno answered. "But if we let him live, then I want more than peace with the son of a bitch. I want him to subject himself to my authority."

"This might help bring that about," Vizzini said.

"What do you think, Nick?" Tangeleno asked Morello.

Morello shook his head. "I would say yes, if we knew we could get the ones who actually killed our men. But to just randomly kill three of his men? What if they are innocent?"

"None of his men are innocent. All right, Sal, kill three of them, then go meet with De Luca and see if he is ready to listen to reason."

Vizzini chuckled. He knew what "listen to reason" meant. When dealing with Tangeleno, those were often the last words a person heard.

"Don Tangeleno, let me go talk to De Luca first," Morello said. "I still think we can work it out."

"You can go talk to him *after* Vizzini takes care of his business," Tangeleno said.

Hawke looked up from the piano keyboard as Vizzini came down the stairs. As usual, Vizzini spoke to no one, nor did he come into the parlor for a drink as many did. Instead he walked straight for the door, opened it, and stepped outside.

A few moments later Evangeline came down the stairs, staying against the wall. When she reached the bottom of the stairs, she kept in the shadows as she went into the kitchen.

When Hawke finished his number, he got up and went into the kitchen, where he poured himself a cup of coffee. Evangeline was sitting back in the corner, wiping away tears as she talked quietly with Doney. They were in the middle of a conversation, so involved that neither of them noticed Hawke when he came in.

"Honey, I know he be a big man in the Family and all, but that don't give him the right to hurt you," Doney was saying.

"You don't understand," Evangeline said.

"I understands, all right. You think he marry you. Maybe I just be a maid, but I got enough sense to know that a man like Vizzini ain' goin' marry no Cajun girl. 'Specially no Cajun girl that be a whore, besides."

"Doney! What a thing to say!" Evangeline said.

Doney reached out to put her hand on Evangeline's. "Honey, I don' mean nothin' bad by what I said. I just want you to know the truth, so's Vizzini don't hurt you no more."

Hawke took a sip of his coffee and studied Evangeline over the rim for a second or two.

"If he treats you like that, why do you have anything to do with him?" Hawke asked.

Evangeline looked up in surprise. She didn't realize that Hawke was in the kitchen and had overheard her conversation with Doney.

"You don't understand," Evangeline said. "He doesn't mean to hurt me, he just gets a little carried away sometimes."

"Would you like me to have a little talk with him?" Hawke asked.

"No no," Evangeline said animatedly. "I mean, it's sweet of you, but. . . ."

"What you are saying is, you don't think he would listen to me?"

"No, I . . . I didn't mean that, exactly. But you are just a piano player and . . . uh," Evangeline started, then she stopped. "I'm sorry, I don't mean any offense."

"No offense taken," Hawke said. He finished his coffee, then put it on the table. "I'd better get back to work," he said.

"Hey, piano player, where you been?" one of the visitors called when Hawke returned. "How 'bout playing some music so as to get some of these women in the mood?"

"Hell, Gus," one of the other men said. "If you can't get a whore in the mood with two dollars, there ain't no music goin' to do it for you."

The parlor erupted in laughter.

Chapter 9

A PIECE OF BREAD LAY ON THE DOCKS, WET AND sodden. A rat, its beady eyes alert for danger, darted out of a warehouse, grabbed the piece of bread, then darted back inside.

In another warehouse Sal Vizzini waited with two other men. He had come here, directly from the whorehouse. It had been good, but the bitch had asked him again: When was he going to marry her? He wished now that he had never mentioned it to her. He only told her that so she would do things for him . . . things that the other girls wouldn't do.

He reached down and rubbed himself. Why couldn't she just leave it alone? There was no way he was going to marry a Cajun, especially *una donnaccia, una prostitute*. If he slapped her around a bit, it was because she needed slapping around.

He rubbed himself again, then got up to look through the crack in the doorway. That was when he saw three of De Luca's men walking up the dock.

"Here they come," Vizzini said.

"We should wait until after they have made their collections," one of the others suggested.

"No," Vizzini replied.

"Come on, think, about it, Vizzini. If we wait until after they make their collections, we can get the money."

"Yeah," the other man with Vizzini said. "That sounds good to me."

Vizzini shook his head emphatically. "If we take the money, De Luca will think that's what this was—just a robbery. He has to understand that this has nothing to do with money."

"*Sí*," the first said. "I agree. *Questo è su onore.* It is about honor."

"Get ready," Vizzini said.

The two men checked the loads in their shotguns, then looked up at Vizzini and nodded that they were ready.

Vizzini went back to the crack in the door, watching as the three men approached.

"You are crazy," one of the three men said, laughing. "A whore is much better than a girlfriend. A whore will do just what you tell her to do."

"But you must pay for it," another said.

"You think you do not pay for it with a girlfriend? She asks you to do this and you do it. She asks you to do that, you do it. No, my friend. You must pay for it, whether it is a whore or a girlfriend. And with a whore, there are no surprises."

The three men laughed.

Suddenly the door of the warehouse was thrown open, and Vizzini and the two men with him stepped out into the open. All three were carrying shotguns.

"*Cosa è questo?*" one of De Luca's three men shouted. "What is this?"

Vizzini and the two men with him opened fire, dealing out death as they stood there, firing from point-blank range at De Luca's men.

There were several dock workers in the area and when the first shot was fired, they added their own screams and shouts to the bedlam as they started running in a mad dash to get out of the way. Some dived for the ground, others ran for cover.

All three of De Luca's men went down, but the firing continued, because as soon as the shotguns were emptied, Vizzini and his men drew their pistols and started firing at the bodies on the ground.

Finally the firing stopped and Vizzini looked down at the three men. One was on his back with a shotgun blast to his chest and another to the side of his head. His face was laced with rivulets of blood.

The other two were lying in a spreading pool of blood.

"Let's go," Vizzini said.

The three men walked away from the riverfront, unchallenged by anyone who remained.

"Tangeleno did this?" De Luca asked Hennesy when the police commissioner brought him the news of the riverfront massacre. "Tangeleno is the one who did the shooting down at the riverfront?"

"Yes," Hennesy said.

"But why?" De Luca asked. "Why would Tangeleno kill three of my men?"

"Because he thinks you killed three of his men," Hennesy said.

"*Quello è matto!* That's crazy! I didn't kill those men," De Luca said.

"If you didn't kill them, who did?" Hennesy asked.

"How the hell would I know?" De Luca snapped back. "I'm not the police here. You are."

"Is it true, what I have heard, that Tangeleno offered to take care of the man who shot Rosario Meli?" Hennesy asked.

"Yes," De Luca replied. "But he was just making a big show. I don't need nor do I want him to fight my battles for me. I know who shot Meli, and I can take care of him any-time I want. The only reason I haven't done it is because Meli deserved what he got. He had no business trying to collect from the grocer. That had nothing to do with us. That was something he was trying to do on his own."

"Do you think it is possible that when Tangeleno sent his men after the person who shot Meli that the same person might have shot them?" Hennesy asked.

De Luca laughed.

"What is so funny?"

"Do you know who you are talking about?"

"I'm talking about the man who shot Meli."

"Do you really think that someone who plays piano in a whorehouse could have killed all three of Tangeleno's men?"

"I don't know. But he did shoot Meli," Hennesy pointed out.

"It was a pure stroke of luck. Meli is a fool, and he wasn't paying attention. He was lucky the piano player didn't kill him."

"You hold no ill will toward the piano player?"

"No," De Luca said. "The piano player was at the grocers, buying groceries for the whores. When Meli shot the grocer, the piano player came to the grocer's defense. That was a thing of honor. I do not kill men for acting in *la questione di onore.*"

"I can understand that."

"Anyway, I do not think the piano player is the one who shot Tangeleno's men."

"Then that brings me back to my original question. If you didn't shoot Tangeleno's men, and if the piano player didn't shoot them, who did?"

"I don't know, I . . ." Stopping in midsentence, De Luca got a strange look on his face and snapped his fingers. "I'll be damned," he said. "I don't know why I didn't think of this be-fore. I know who killed Tangeleno's men."

"Who?"

"Tangeleno did it."

"What?" Hennesy asked, surprised by De Luca's sugges-tion. "Why would he do something like that?"

"Because he wants to start a war," De Luca explained. "Or at least he wants to push us to the brink of a war. He shot his own men so he could blame me for it, then he used that as an excuse to kill three of my men."

Hennesy shook his head. "I don't know . . . That seems pretty far-fetched to me."

"Now he is going to make a big show of trying to make peace between us. He'll send someone to talk to me, to try and convince me that the only way we can have peace is if I accept his offer to merge our organizations. The only ques-tion is: Who will he use to make contact with me?"

Hennesy stroked his chin for a long moment. "Oh shit."

"What is it?"

"The son of a bitch is using me," Hennesy said.

"What do you mean, he's using you?"

"Tangeleno came to see me. He asked me to bring you a message. He wants to send someone over to talk peace with you."

"Why would Tangeleno come see you, Hennesy? Are you working for him now?"

"No, De Luca, no, I'm not," Hennesy said quickly. "I guess he thought I was the best way to get through to you."

"That makes sense, I guess, since he knows that I am pay-ing you money."

"What? How does he know that?" Hennesy asked, his face registering alarm.

"I told him."

"De Luca, no! Why did you do that? It is not good that he knows. It's not good for either one of us."

"You don't understand the way things work with us, Hen-nesy. He needs to know that I have *collegamenti potenti*."

"I beg your pardon? I don't speak Italian."

"I said he needs to know that I have powerful connections," De Luca translated.

"I don't like it. I don't like being pulled into the middle of all this."

"You are already in the middle of it. You got in the middle of it the first time you took money from me. Now, what is the message?" De Luca asked.

"He wants to send Morello to set up a meeting between you and Tangeleno."

"Morello, huh?"

"Yes."

"Morello is his number-two man. He must really think he has me where he wants me. All right, tell him he can send Morello," De Luca said.

"Can I tell him you will guarantee Morello's safety?" Hennesy asked.

De Luca looked at Hennesy. "Tell him to send Morello," he said pointedly.

Chapter 10

HAWKE WALKED THROUGH THE FRENCH DOORS of his apartment to stand out on the veranda. As part of his compensation, Clarisse had provided him with an apartment on the second floor of the House of the Evening Star. His room was on the same floor as the *chambres des dames de plaisir*, the rooms of the ladies of pleasure. He was guaranteed his privacy because he was separated from the women and their "working rooms," by a wall that had no door. In order to get to his room from the business part of the building, one would have to go down one set of stairs and come up to his room by another.

Hawke smiled as he contemplated his living arrangements. In all his travels, this was the first time he had ever lived in a whorehouse.

Resting his elbows on the wrought-iron grillwork railing that extended across the front of his balcony, Hawke looked out over the city. He couldn't help but be impressed by nighttime New Orleans. The lights were as bright now as they had been on the night he arrived by train. The Crescent City was illuminated by the flickering lamps that lined the streets, as well as the several yellow squares of light that were cast through the windows of the many restaurants, homes, and establishments.

From downstairs, he heard the *pop* of a champagne cork, then an explosion of laughter. As Big Callie suggested, Hawke had found much about New Orleans to like. The city certainly had its cultural side, with traveling dramatic groups playing in the local theaters, as well as an excellent symphony orchestra, and a very good ballet company.

But he had also discovered a more sinister side. Much of New Orleans seemed to be controlled by a shadowy group of outlaws. And, while Hawke had encountered outlaws before, even gangs of outlaws, he had never run across anything quite like the Mafia.

He could relate to being shot at, though. And Hawke decided that being a target was little different, whether you were being shot at by a Yankee sniper in the war, a Texas horse thief, or a Sicilian Mafioso.

But Hawke had been in New Orleans for six weeks. He came here because he wanted to see New Orleans. Well, he had seen it, and now he was ready to move on. To that end, he had told Clarisse, earlier this week, that he would be leaving soon.

"I hate to see you go," Clarisse replied, disappointed at hearing his announcement. "But I have to admit that you did warn me you wouldn't stick around very long."

"It has been an interesting six weeks," Hawke said. "But I'm ready to see what's over the nearest hill."

Clarisse laughed. "Oh, honey, it's a long way from New Orleans to the nearest hill," she said.

"That's right," Hawke said, pointedly.

Clarisse sighed. "Well, you have been a wonderful asset to our place of business, Mason, and I also like to think you have become a good friend. I wish you luck."

"Thanks."

That conversation had taken place three days earlier. This was Hawke's last night at the House of the Evening Star. Tomorrow, he would be departing for St. Louis, Missouri, onboard a Mississippi riverboat, *Delta Mist*, having been hired to play piano in the great salon.

This wasn't to be a longtime job either, because once the boat reached St. Louis, Hawke planned to board a train and head west. He had no specific destination in mind, as long as it was somewhere in the West.

Finishing his glass of wine, Hawke went back into his apartment, put on an emerald jacket, adjusted his yellow cravat, and went downstairs to work.

"There you are, you handsome devil, you," Clarisse said as Hawke stepped into the parlor.

Clarisse was a little younger than her sister, Big Callie, had been. She was also considerably smaller, though she wasn't a petite woman by any means. Her blonde hair was piled in ringlets on top of her head and her low-cut gown displayed a generous spill of creamy white breasts.

"You have come to break our hearts one last night, have you?"

"Clarisse, you could always give this up and run away with me," Hawke teased.

"Oh, don't think for one minute I wouldn't do it if I thought you were serious," Clarisse said.

Hawke laughed. "And abandon your girls? You know you are their mother, and they are your children. You couldn't leave them."

"Maybe not," Clarisse said. "But oh, I will have a wonderful time fantasizing about it. Hawke, as a special favor for me on your last night, would you play 'Beautiful Dreamer'?"

"I would be honored," Hawke said.

* * *

Clarisse watched Hawke walk through the parlor, exchanging pleasantries with the women and their customers. She chuckled as she recalled a notion she had shared with the other girls, shortly after Hawke arrived. Clarisse had told the girls that if she could find four or five more men who were as handsome and refined as Hawke, she could start a brothel for women.

"Of course, I'm sure I would be tarred, feathered, and run out of town," she admitted. "I don't think New Orleans is ready for such an arrangement yet, but I do believe it would do very well."

Taking his seat at the piano, Hawke began playing, starting out with Clarisse's request. When he finished, he looked toward her, smiled, and nodded his head. Returning his smile, Clarisse gave him a slight curtsey.

"It *is* you," a man said, coming up to the piano.

Turning, Hawke saw a small man, nearly bald, with round cheeks and prominent ears. Although Hawke showed no sign of recognition, he knew who the man was.

"Something I can play for you?" Hawke said.

"It is you, isn't it?"

Hawke chuckled. "As far as I know, I am me."

"That's not what I mean. I am Professor Leonard Tompkins," the man said. "And if I am not mistaken, you and I once shared the billing at Vienna's *Grosser Musikvereinssall*. You *are* that Mason Hawke, aren't you?"

"That was a long time ago," Hawke said.

Tompkins smiled broadly. "I knew it!" He hit his fist into his hand. "I knew it!"

"How are you doing, Professor?"

"I'm doing fine, just fine. Wonderfully, in fact," the professor replied. "I am the conductor of the New Orleans Symphony Orchestra," he added proudly.

"Good for you," Hawke said.

"I don't understand," Tompkins said.

"What is it you don't understand?"

Professor Tompkins looked around the room at the scantily clad women and their customers. "I don't understand why you are here," he said.

Hawke laughed. "Well, as you can see, Professor, I'm playing the piano. But a better question might be what are *you* doing here?"

Tompkins cleared his throat. "Oh well, uh, see here, this is rather embarrassing," he said. "But I hasten to add that I am a widower, so it isn't as if I am cheating or anything."

Hawke chuckled and held up his hand. "You misunderstand me, Professor," he said. "I'm not passing judgment on you. I'm not qualified to pass judgment on anyone for anything."

"Where have you been for the last . . . what has it been? Sixteen, seventeen years since our European tour?"

"Something like that," Hawke replied, without answering the rest of the question. "By the way, you should be congratulated. You have a very good symphony orchestra," Hawke said.

"You've attended some of our concerts then?"

"Yes."

"I don't mean to be vain, but, didn't you recognize my name? Didn't you remember our sharing the bill?"

"Yes," Hawke said. "I knew who you were."

"Well, man, why didn't you come to see me? I would have put you on with the orchestra immediately. In fact, I would feature you."

Hawke shook his head. "I don't do that anymore," he said.

"What do you mean, you don't do that anymore? You are doing it now."

"No, I'm playing piano in a whorehouse," he said. "It isn't the same thing."

"No, not exactly, but . . ."

"I thank you for your offer," Hawke said, cutting him off. "But I don't do that anymore."

Tompkins stood there for a moment longer before realizing that Hawke was serious, that he wasn't just trying to elicit further response or a more specific offer.

"All right," Tompkins said. "I don't understand why you feel that way, but I'll respect your decision. But if you ever do change your mind, if you would like to get back into serious music again, please, come see me."

"Thank you. I do appreciate your offer," Hawke said again.

Chapter 11

DE LUCA WAS SITTING AT A TABLE ON THE POR-
tico at the back of his house, sipping a glass of wine as he
read the *New Orleans Picayune*.

MORE VIOLENCE
AMONG THE ITALIANS

On the 4th, Instant, there was a nighttime gun
battle in which three Italians were found
gunned down in an empty lot in the 1100 block
of Dauphine Street. These three were said to be
members of the Innocents, known to be controlled by Joseph Tangeleno.

It is believed that they were killed by members of Carlos De Luca's associates, known as
the Family, and indeed, but one week following,
three members of De Luca's Family were murdered on the riverfront.

Although many citizens have called upon the
city government to take whatever action is required to rid our city of this scourge, to date, the

city has refused to act. Some have suggested
that members of the city government, including
the police, may be involved by way of receiving
graft payments from one or more of these criminal elements.

"Don De Luca?"

De Luca looked up from his newspaper and saw Provenzano.

"Yes?"

"Morello is here," Provenzano said.

"Did he come alone?"

"Yes."

"Is everything ready?" De Luca asked.

"Yes."

De Luca folded his newspaper and lay it aside. "Very well,
tell the others. Then bring him back here."

Chapter 12

RACHEL WAS LOOKING AT A FIELD OF FLOWERS, blue bachelor's buttons, yellow black-eyed Susans, orange butterfly weeds, and cardinal flowers that were a brilliant red. The flowers moved gently to and fro in the breeze, causing the colors to meld and join together in one giant patchwork quilt.

The windmill answered a breeze and, as the blades began spinning, she could hear a squeaking sound.

The squeak got louder and more insistent and the pictures in her mind drifted away. The squeaking windmill was replaced by the squeaking sound of her bed. The flowers were gone too, and in their stead she saw the flocked wallpaper of her room.

"Uhnn!" the man who was thrusting against her said. "Uhn, uhn, uhn, ohhhhhh!"

He stopped his thrusting, the bed stopped squeaking, and he lay on her with all his weight, breathing hard.

"Honey," Rachel said quietly. "Honey, you're weighing me down." She pushed against him, insistently, but not too aggressively.

"Oh yeah," he said. He rolled off of her, then lay in the bed beside her, still breathing hard. "Damn, that was good."

"Oh, I'm so glad you liked it."

Rachel's client was a man named Pietro Franchetti. She knew that he was Italian and was connected in some way with De Luca, but she didn't know all the ins and outs of the Sicilian groups who so controlled New Orleans.

They lay side by side for a few minutes longer before Rachel spoke again. "Pietro, I'm going to have to get on back downstairs now," she said.

"All right."

Pietro sat up, then reached for his pants. He laughed. "I didn't bother to put on my underdrawers because I knew I was comin' here tonight."

"That sounds like a smart move to me," Rachel said.

From the room next to hers, Rachael heard a popping sound, then a cry.

She slipped into a robe, then walked to the door.

"I wouldn't open the door if I were you," Pietro said.

Rachel looked back toward him.

"You don't want to get involved with someone like Sal Vizzini," Pietro said.

"Why is he like that?" Rachel asked. "Why is he so cruel?"

"It is not good to ask such things," Pietro replied.

Rachel heard another popping sound and another cry.

"Please . . . don't," she heard. She recognized Evangeline's voice, even though it was muffled and filled with pain.

"Shut up, bitch," she heard Vizzini say. "I've bought and paid for you. You'll do any damn thing I want."

Hawke was passing by the bottom of the stairs, carrying a cup of coffee he had just gotten from the kitchen, when he heard the exchange. Stopping, he looked up toward the top of the stairs and waited for a moment.

"You said that if I let you come back, you wouldn't hurt me anymore," he heard Evangeline say. "You promised."

He heard a man's laughter. "Since when does a promise made to a whore mean anything?"

"It's Evangeline," Clarisse said when she saw Hawke standing at the foot of the stairs.

Hawke nodded. "Yes, I know. It's Vizzini again, isn't it?"

"I'm afraid so. He is such an evil person."

"Maybe someone should have a talk with him," Hawke suggested.

"Yes, but who would have the courage?" Clarisse asked.

Hawke returned to his piano, but he kept a close eye on the stairs. When he saw Vizzini coming down the stairs, he cut his song short, in order to keep an eye on Evangeline's abuser. Then, when Vizzini went out the front door, Hawke stepped out the back.

The night creatures were singing as Hawke stood in the gazebo, waiting. The dark air was warm, moist, and malodorous with the stench of the outhouse that sat back in the corner.

As he knew he would, Vizzini headed toward the outhouse to relieve himself before he started home. Hawke waited until he unbuttoned his pants, then Hawke suddenly stepped behind him and grabbed him.

"Here!" Vizzini said in sharp fear. "What are you doing?"

"I'm throwing your ass in the toilet," Hawke said in a hissing whisper.

"What? Do you know who I am?"

"I know exactly who you are, Vizzini," Hawke said. "You are a piece of shit."

Hawke grabbed Vizzini by the scruff of his neck and the seat of his pants. With one powerful lift, he picked Vizzini up.

"What are you . . . arrrghh!" Vizzini shouted, though his final words were mumbled when his head was submerged in the honey bucket beneath the only hole of the one-hole toilet.

Chapter 13

BACK INSIDE THE HOUSE, CLARISSE AND THE OTHers were blissfully unaware of what had just taken place outside. When Hawke came back in, Clarisse assumed that he had just stepped out for a little air or perhaps to use the toilet. Hawke went immediately to the piano and started playing again.

Clarisse was standing at the foot of the stairs when Rachel came down. The height of the evening had not yet been reached, and there were still several men and women in the parlor.

"Good evening, Clarisse," Rachel said as she passed the madam of the house.

"Good evening, Rachel. How did it go with Mr. Franchetti?"

"He seemed well satisfied," Rachel said.

Clarisse stared at Rachel for a long moment. "Honey, why do you do this kind of work if you hate it so?"

"I've never said I hated it," Rachel replied.

Clarisse put her hand on Rachel's neck and squeezed it gently. "You don't have to say it, dear. It's written on your face like a book."

"Oh," Rachel said. "I'm sorry. I hope the men don't think . . ."

Clarisse interrupted her with a laugh. "Honey, men don't think. Period," she said. "When a beautiful girl like you spreads her legs for them, all their thoughts and feelings are in one place."

Rachel laughed with her.

"I understand you got a letter from Louise."

"Yes, a couple of weeks ago."

"How is she doing?"

"She's doing fine."

"I'm real glad about that. I miss her. She was a sweet girl."

Suddenly the front door opened and Vizzini stepped inside. He let out a loud yell.

"Who did this?" he shouted angrily. His sudden entrance brought all other activity to a halt and everyone looked toward the front door. Vizzini was covered with an odorous brown sludgelike substance.

"My God! What the hell did you fall into?" someone near the door shouted. By now, the stench was permeating the entire parlor.

"I want to know who threw me into the toilet!" Vizzini shouted.

For a moment there was a stunned silence, then someone laughed out loud and that broke the ice for the others. The parlor roared with laughter.

"Don't you laugh!" Vizzini shouted, pointing to the parlor. "Don't you sons of bitches laugh!"

Despite their fear of him, the laughter continued unabated, and Vizzini stood there for a moment longer, fuming in anger and humiliation. Then, realizing that he was the object of their ridicule, he turned and hurried out of the parlor, chased by the howling laughter and catcalls of the men and women of the House of the Evening Star.

"Whew," Clarisse said, fanning her hand under her nose. "Would some of you please open the windows so we can get some air in here? Doney, please come and clean this up."

"Yes, ma'am, I be right there," Doney replied, hurrying toward the front door with a bucket and some rags. "It be a pleasure to clean this up after seein' that man get his comeuppance," she added, laughing.

"All right, ladies and gentlemen, the disturbance is over. Let's settle down now," Clarisse called. "Mr. Hawke, would you play for us, please?"

"It will be my pleasure."

"And if you would, dedicate the song to whoever the stalwart soul was who pushed Vizzini into the toilet."

Hawke chuckled. "Yes, ma'am," he said. "That will be my pleasure as well."

Rachel walked through the parlor to sit on the sofa nearest the piano so she could listen to the music. The music wasn't the only reason she chose to sit here. She sat here because she wanted to be close to Hawke.

Ever since he arrived, Hawke had been polite to her; but then he was polite to all the girls. And he was never judgmental, nor patronizing. But Rachel was disappointed because, although she had recognized him right away, he still hadn't recognized her.

To be fair to him, she realized there was no real reason he should recognize her. After all, it had been a very long time since they last saw each other, and she had been much younger then.

She recalled the last time she had seen him, dashingly handsome then, as now. Then, however, he had been wearing the gray and gold uniform of a regiment of Confederate cavalry.

She didn't think she had ever seen anyone as handsome,

nor had there ever been anything as exciting as watching the county regiment marching off under fluttering flags to do battle for Georgia and the Confederate States of America.

"Oh, Mama, I pray that nothing happens to father and to Mason Hawke while they are off fighting in the war."

"But, Rachel, you should pray for all of our brave young men, not just father and Mason Hawke. You should also pray for Mason Hawke's brother and father, as well as all of the other soldiers in the regiment."

"Oh, I do, Mama. I do pray for all of them," Rachel said. "And I feel guilty."

Rachel's mother laughed. "Why do you feel guilty?"

"Because they will be in such danger while we will be safe at home."

"That is the nature of war, my dear. The men go off to do battle and the women stay home to pray for them."

As it turned out, Rachel was not as safe as she thought she would be. The war had been going on for four long years on the night six Yankee soldiers smashed down the door and came into the house. After taking what little food remained, the six men took turns raping Rachel and her mother.

Afterward, as Rachel lay bleeding and hurting in a crumpled heap over in the corner, the youngest of the soldiers came over to talk to her. He had a pained look of contrition on his face and he tried to offer her a piece of cornbread.

Pulling her quilt more tightly around her, Rachel drew away from him, looking at him through large, hurt, and terrified eyes. She refused the cornbread.

"I'm sorry," the young soldier said. He sighed and looked over his shoulder at the other five men, who, by now, were throwing out their bedrolls on the living room floor.

"Normally, this ain't the way we are," the boy soldier said.

"I mean, we're good people. We ain't really like this. I don't know what . . . uh . . . that is, we ain't never done nothin' like this before."

The young soldier pointed to the soldier who had stripes on his sleeve. "Sergeant Miller there, well, he's married and has two kids. He's a mechanic. Gibson is a farmer. And them other two boys works in a mill. Me, well, I just got out of school."

Rachel said nothing.

"Anyway," the young soldier continued. "I been prayin' to the Lord to forgive me for what we . . . I mean, for what I done to you and your ma. This war, it makes . . ."—he stopped in midsentence and sighed. "Well, I don't expect you to find it in your heart to forgive me," he said. "But I do want you to know that I'm sorry."

The soldiers left the next morning without forcing themselves on Rachel or her mother a second time. Rachel couldn't find it in her heart to forgive them, but she did adjust to what happened to her.

Her mother never did adjust and wasn't "quite right" after that. Rachel's father had died of dysentery shortly after the war began and, though she prayed for forgiveness for such thoughts, Rachel was glad that her father had not lived to see her mother this way.

Rachel took care of her mother as best she could, but within two years of the war's end, her mother was dead and Rachel found herself without a farm and with no place to go. In order to support herself, she took a job in the laundry. One of her coworkers was Sally, a young black girl who had once been a slave of her family. It was from Sally that Rachel learned about the House of the Evening Star.

"It's in New Orleans, and my sister works there," Sally said after she told Rachel about it.

"Your sister? Are you talking about Fancy? Our Fancy?"

Like Sally, Fancy had been one of her family's slaves.

"Yes'm, that be the one I'm talkin' about, all right. You might remember, Fancy be a shine."

Calling Fancy a "shine," Rachel knew, referred to the fact that she was very light-skinned.

"And Fancy say that the New Orleans gentlemens likes the light-skin Coloreds almost as much as they like the white girls. She say it's a real nice place too, the girls is treated real good and they makes lots of money."

"They make a lot of money? How much money is a lot of money?" Rachel asked.

"Fancy say she make a hundred dollars a month," Sally said.

Rachel gasped in amazement. "A hundred dollars a month? Lord, I didn't know there was so much money in the world."

"You could make that much money," Sally said. "You be a real pretty girl. I expect lots of men would pay money to be with you."

"Sally, are you suggesting that I become a prostitute?"

"No, ma'am, I ain't suggestin' nothin'. I'm just tellin' you that you could make lots of money doin' that if you wanted to."

At first Rachel thought she should be angry with Sally, but the more she thought about it, the better the idea sounded to her. And why not? She wasn't entitled to any pride or shame anyway. That had been taken from her, along with her innocence when she was raped by the Yankee soldiers.

"But how would I ever get on there?" Rachel asked. "I mean, if there is that much money to be made, I'm sure there are many who apply for the position."

"If you go see Fancy, she help you get on," Sally said.

"Fancy might be your sister, but she was one of our slaves. Why would she be willing to help me?" Rachel asked.

"'Cause she be your sister too," Sally said.

"What?" Rachel asked in shock. "Fancy is my sister? But how is that possible?"

Sally laughed. "Miss Rachel, if you don' know how babies is borned, you ain't goin' be much good as a whore, no matter how pretty you is."

"I know how babies are born," Rachel said. "I just don't know how it is that Fancy could be my sister."

"'Cause your daddy visit my mama from time to time," Sally said.

"I . . . I never knew."

"No, ma'am, I don't reckon they was many folks what know'd, bein' as your daddy and my mama was quiet about it. But your daddy know'd and from time to time he would come down and bounce Fancy on his knee and tell her that she was just as purty as a little pair of red shoes."

Rachel gasped. "As 'pretty as a little pair of red shoes'? That's what my father would say to Fancy?"

"That's what he said, all right."

"Why that . . . that's exactly what he used to say to me," Rachel said. "Oh my, it is true! He was Fancy's father. She is my sister."

Armed with a letter from Sally, Rachel went to New Orleans, where Fancy not only helped her get a job with the House of the Evening Star, but received her so warmly that the two half-sisters became very close friends.

Now, as Rachel sat on the sofa near the piano listening to the music, her half-sister came over to sit with her.

Fancy was an exceptionally beautiful girl with copper-toned skin, large dark eyes with big fanlike eyelashes, high cheekbones, and luxuriant black hair. As a result of her exotic beauty, she was one of the most sought-after girls in the house.

"Are you going to tell him?" Fancy asked.

"No."

"I think you should tell him who you are," Fancy urged.

"No, I can't," Rachel answered.

"Why not? He's leaving tomorrow. If you don't tell him now, Rachel, he's never going to know."

"It's better this way."

"Why is it better this way?"

"Fancy, do you think I want him to know I'm a whore?"

Fancy laughed. "Rachel, he works here. He *knows* you are a whore."

"Yes, but he doesn't know who I am."

"If you don't tell him, I'm going to," Fancy insisted. She started to stand.

"Fancy, no, please, don't!" Rachel said, reaching out to pull her back. Rachel's plea was so sincere that Fancy acquiesced.

"All right, if you don't want me to tell him, I won't," she said, sitting back down.

"Thank you."

"But you're crazy," Fancy said. "You know that, don't you? A man like that and you know him from the past, but you don't say anything about it. I sure can't understand that."

"Rachel?" a man's voice said.

Looking up from the sofa, Rachel saw a small balding man.

"Professor Tompkins," she said, flashing a sweet smile at him. "How good to see you tonight."

"Do you think we could, uh, go upstairs?" Tompkins asked, almost embarrassed by the asking.

"Why, of course we can," Rachel replied. "I would be delighted to spend some time with you."

As Rachel and Professor Tompkins started toward the stairs, they passed a man of medium height, with dark hair and dark blue eyes. He was wearing a hat with a small round crown and a small brim. He lifted it by way of greeting Rachel.

"Hello, Mr. Provenzano," Rachel said.

Professor Tompkins looked away pointedly, as if trying to avoid recognition.

"I enjoyed your last concert, Professor," Provenzano said. "I like Rossini. You should play more Italian composers."

Professor Tompkins held his left hand up, as if shielding his face.

"Yes, uh, thank you," he mumbled.

Provenzano laughed at the professor's embarrassment, then walked over to Fancy. "Fancy, *buona sera,*" he said.

"Vinnie," Fancy said, smiling coquettishly at him. "I thought you said you had a meeting and you weren't going to come tonight."

"I did. But the meeting didn't last long," Vinnie said.

"It didn't go well?"

"You might say that the man I met with lost his head," Vinnie said with an ironic chuckle.

Chapter 14

❦

TANGELENO WAS ON THE BACK PORCH CAREFULLY
trimming and working on his orchid plants when Sal Vizzini
stepped out onto the back porch.

Tangeleno put his hand on the orchid and held the petals
out so Vizzini could see them. "This is the Vanda Limbata,"
he said. "Isn't it beautiful?"

"Yeah, beautiful," Vizzini said.

Tangeleno sniffed, then sniffed again before realizing that
the smell was coming from Vizzini.

"What the hell? Are you wearing perfume?"

"Yeah, I, uh, had a little accident," Vizzini said. "I took a
bath, but I could still smell it, so I put on a little perfume."

Tangeleno chuckled. "Just so long as you don't turn
strange on me."

"Huh, you don't have to worry about anything like that,"
Vizzini said.

"What do you want, Sal? You don't normally come out
here just to enjoy my flowers."

"Nick Morello's carriage has returned," Vizzini said.

Tangeleno squinted his eyes in curiosity. "What do you mean, Nick's carriage? Not Nick?"

"I think maybe you should come into the parlor," Vizzini suggested.

Putting down his trowel and scissors, Tangeleno moved quickly into the parlor. There, three of his men were standing, waiting for him.

"What is it?" Tangeleno said. "What's going on here?"

One of the men pointed to a wicker box. The lid was closed.

"What is that?" Tangeleno asked.

"This was on the seat of Nick's carriage," one of the men said.

"What's in it?"

"We don't know what is in it, Don Tangeleno," Vizzini said. "We thought we would wait until you saw it, before we opened it."

"All right, I'm here. Open it," Tangeleno said.

Vizzini nodded to the man standing nearest the box. He released the clasp, opened the lid, then stepped back with a gasp.

"Well?" Tangeleno demanded. "What is it?"

"I . . . I think you should look, Don Tangeleno," the man said.

Tangeleno stepped up to the box and looked down inside. Like the man who had opened it, Tangeleno gasped.

There, inside the box, was the severed head of Nicholas Morello.

"Nicholas, oh, Nicholas, my friend," Tangeleno said in a choked voice. He stared at the head for a long moment, then turned to Vizzini. "You say his carriage brought this back? No driver?"

"The gardener saw the equipage coming in without a driver, so he moved out front to halt the horses and investigate. That was when he saw the box and brought it in. There was no message from De Luca."

"Oh yes. Yes, there was a message from De Luca," Tangeleno said. He pointed to the head. "This was his message."

"How could De Luca do such a thing?" Vizzini asked, shaking his head sadly.

"I want him dead," Tangeleno said. "I want De Luca and Provenzano dead. I want everyone who works for them dead. I want their soldiers dead, I want their servants dead. And if he has any dogs, cats, or goldfish, I want them dead too!" Tangeleno said, ending with a loud shout.

"*Sí, sara, Don Tangeleno,*" Vizzini said. "It will be," Vizzini promised.

Chapter 15

THE *DELTA MIST* LEFT HER MOORING PLACE BEFORE dawn the next morning and moved over to one of the boarding docks in order to facilitate passenger loading. Prospective passengers were advised by circulars and by advertisements that had been placed in the city newspaper to "board between the hours of seven and nine in the morning."

Hawke had never been on a riverboat before, and he watched with interest as the passengers began to stream aboard.

"Oh, Papa, look how big this boat is!" one little boy exclaimed as he stepped onboard with his family. "Why, I bet this is the biggest boat in the whole world!"

"I wouldn't say that," the boy's father replied. "But it certainly is a nice big boat."

The boy's mother looked around and held on to her husband's arm, and Hawke could read in her face the changing expression of all her feelings: excitement, hope, fear, determination, and courage. Seeing families like that sometimes made Hawke realize how shallow and empty his own life was, and, cursing himself for such thoughts, he turned away from the loading passengers.

"Sorry, sir," a deckhand said. "But passengers aren't allowed on this part of the deck."

"I'm not a passenger," Hawke replied. "I'm a crewman."

The deckhand looked at Hawke, clearly not believing him. "You say you are a new crewman?"

"I'm a crewman in a manner of speaking," Hawke replied.

"What do you mean, 'a manner of speaking'?"

"I'm Mason Hawke, the new pianist."

"The new what?"

"I'll be playing piano in the grand salon," Hawke explained. "At least until we reach St. Louis."

"A piano player?" the deckhand said. "Well, yes, sir, I reckon that does make you a crew member." He stuck his hand out. "The name is John Lee, and I welcome you aboard the *Delta Mist*."

"I'm happy to be aboard," Hawke said.

About half an hour later, with all passengers aboard, the captain pulled on the chain that blew the boat whistle and its deep-throated tones could be heard all up and down the river.

The captain put the engine in reverse and the steam boomed out of the steam-relief pipe like the firing of a cannon. The stern wheel began spinning in reverse and the boat pulled away from the dock, then turned with the stern pointing downriver and the bow pointing upstream. The engine lever was slipped to full forward, and the wheel began spinning in the other direction until it finally caught hold, overcame the force of the current, and started moving the boat upstream.

Hawke stood on the deck watching the dock fall away as the boat beat its way against the current, then negotiated the wide, sweeping bend that gave the Crescent City its name.

The engine steam pipe continued to boom loudly, as if the city were under a cannonading.

In midstream now, the *Delta Mist* started working its way upriver, with its two engines clattering and the paddle wheel slapping and the boat itself being enveloped in the thick smoke that belched out from the high twin stacks.

The sound of the boat whistle and the booming of the steam pipe rolled across the city, awakening Rachel. Opening her eyes, she lay with her head on the pillow for a moment or two, enjoying the very bright sun that streamed in through the window, illuminating the room.

She thought about the boat and wondered if that was the boat that Hawke was on. Perhaps Fancy had been right. Maybe she should have told him who she was. As it stood now, they were never going to see each other again anyway. It might have been interesting to reach back in time—if just for a moment or two.

To her surprise, she felt a lump in her throat and tears in her eyes.

"This is ridiculous," she said aloud. "What did I think he would do, even if I had told him? I did the right thing."

"Mary! Mary, you get those clothes hung up on the line, do you hear me?"

"Yes, Mama, I'm doing it now," a young girl's voice answered.

The voices were coming from outside, drifting into the room on the soft breeze that filled the muslin curtains at the slightly raised window and lifted them, cloudlike, over the carpeted floor.

Rachel heard the little girl singing a cheery morning song and she got out of bed and walked over to the window to look down onto the alley. She saw a young girl of about twelve, hanging a wash on the line. Mary lived in the house that was just across the alley behind the House of the Evening Star.

Rachel lifted the window all the way up. "Good morning, Mary," Rachel called down to her.

"Good morning, Miss Rachel," Mary called back.

"Mary!" her mother scolded from inside the house. "I've told you not to talk to any of those women."

"But, Mama, Miss Rachel is my friend."

"Women like that are friends of no one, except Satan," the woman said.

Stung by the harsh words, Rachel put the window down, then looked at the clock. It was ten o'clock, and she knew that most of the city had been awake for several hours now. The house had been quite busy last night, and after Professor Tompkins, she had entertained two more men. But it was very quiet this morning, and that made it conducive to sleeping late.

Rachel got dressed and stepped out into the hallway. When she did so, she saw Doney folding towels and sheets and stacking them on shelves in a hall closet. Rachel smiled. She remembered wondering, when she first arrived, how one place could use as many towels as this place did. That curiosity had been one of the last vestiges of her naïveté. She had been here for over two years now. She had experienced many men, in many different ways, and by now there was no curiosity left unfulfilled.

The door across from Rachel's room opened and Fancy stepped out into the hall, yawning and stretching.

"Good morning, Fancy," Rachel said.

"Good morning, Rachel," Fancy replied. "Did you have a busy night?"

"Not too busy," Rachel replied. "How about you?"

"Just Vinnie, but he stayed all night," Fancy said. She

turned to the maid. "Doney, I had to come down here and get my own towel last night." She brushed her hand through her hair to push the strands back away from her face.

"The towels was here, wasn't they?" the older woman answered. "I brung 'em in from the line and folded 'em. I just hadn't gotten around to puttin' 'em in the rooms yet."

"Yes, but I don't want to have to come get them, Doney, I want them in my room," Fancy said. "I thought we had an understanding. We spread our legs for the men, you keep us supplied with clean towels."

"I just be one person, Fancy," Doney said, walking away in a huff.

Fancy turned to Rachel, who had been watching everything in amused curiosity.

"I tell you, sometimes that woman can be pure mean-spirited," Fancy said. Her comment, however, was ameliorated with a smile.

"Doney's all right," Rachel said. "And she is overworked."

"Don't ever let her hear you say that she's overworked. Lord, we'll never get another lick of work out of her," Fancy said, laughing.

"Fancy? Fancy, I must be going," someone called from the room with the open door. A man followed the voice, stepping out into the hallway. He was still wearing his hat with a small round crown and a small brim, but he was wearing absolutely nothing else.

"Hello, Mr. Provenzano," Rachel said.

"Rachel," Provenzano said, lifting his hat. When the maid came back, bringing more towels, Provenzano spoke to her. "Doney, did you get my clothes washed?"

Provenzano showed no more concern over being naked in front of the maid than he had being naked in front of Rachel and Fancy.

"Yes, sir, Mr. Provenzano," Doney answered, and she

pointed to a table where freshly laundered underwear, shirt, and pants lay.

"Thanks," Provenzano said.

Smiling, Rachel went back into her room to make up her bed. She was just finishing when there was a light knock.

"Yes?" she said.

"It's Provenzano."

Rachel opened the door and saw Provenzano standing there. He was still wearing his hat, but now he was fully dressed.

"I would like to invite you and Fancy to a dinner tonight, to be hosted by Don Carlos De Luca. The dinner will be at his home."

"Oh, I don't know."

"I realize we will have to pay for your time. I'll clear it with Clarisse."

Looking over Provenzano's shoulder, Rachel saw Fancy standing behind him.

"What do you think, Fancy?" she asked.

"I think it will be great fun," Fancy said. "Oh, do say that you will go."

"All right," Rachel agreed. "I'll go."

"Good!" Fancy said, clapping her hands in delight.

"Where is Mr. De Luca's house?" Rachel asked.

"You don't have to worry about that," Provenzano said. "I'll send a carriage down to pick you up."

Chapter 16

HUMMINGBIRDS FLITTED AROUND THE CREPE MYR-
tle bush, darting from bloom to bloom. Near the bush was the
alabaster statue of a nude woman holding a basin. The basin,
which was filled with water, gave the birds a place to drink
and bathe. Throughout the garden, flowers bloomed in color-
ful profusion.

Carlos De Luca's backyard was one of the showcase lawns
of New Orleans. The grass was well manicured and kept free
of weeds, the lawn was terraced, beautifully landscaped, and
filled with statuary of all sizes and shapes. There was also a
large round pool, crowned by a very ornate fountain. De
Luca was clearly proud of his yard, and when Rachel and
Fancy arrived earlier in the evening, he showed it off with
great relish.

Rachel responded to the show with the proper enthusiasm
and enjoyment, though in truth she thought that the many
statues, birdbaths, fountains, and pools made the garden a little too extravagant for her tastes.

Although some of Rachel's clients had taken her to dinner

at restaurants from time to time, this was the very first time she had ever been to a private home, and she commented about it to Fancy.

"Oh, I've been in private homes many times," Fancy replied.

"You have?"

"Yes."

"Why, that's wonderful."

"Not so wonderful."

"What do you mean?"

"Don't you know why I'm never taken to a restaurant?"

"No."

"Think about it, Rachel. I'm colored."

"But you are only half-colored."

Fancy laughed. "That might be true, but I haven't been able to figure out how to separate the white half that they will let into the restaurants from the colored half that has to stay outside."

Rachel laughed with her.

"To be honest, Fancy, I sometimes forget that you are colored. I never think of you that way anymore. I just think of you as my friend—and my sister."

As the two young women surveyed the garden, they walked around the backyard in their butterfly-bright gowns, almost as if a couple of the flowers themselves had come alive. Provenzano asked them to wear their most beautiful gowns and, acquiescing to the request, Rachel was wearing a bright yellow gown, while Fancy chose lavender.

"This is a celebration," Provenzano told them when he issued the invitation.

"What sort of celebration?"

"Fifteen years ago, on this date, our Sicilian brotherhood overthrew the Bourbon authority in Palermo."

"Oh, then it is like your Independence Day," Rachel said.

"Yeah," Provenzano replied. "You might say it is something like that."

They would be dining outside in the garden and, even as the women strolled around enjoying the garden, unaware that, by their beauty they were actually a part of the scenery, servants hovered about as they prepared for the meal.

They weren't ordinary servants, though. As Provenzano explained, someone like De Luca could not afford to have ordinary servants because it would be too dangerous. Therefore all his servants were Sicilian soldiers.

"Soldiers? You mean like in the army?" Rachel asked.

"Sort of like that, only this isn't the U.S. Army. This is more like Don De Luca's private army."

Whether servants or soldiers, they knew their jobs and they did them well. The dining room table was covered with a damask tablecloth and set with glistening china, sparkling crystal, and shining silver.

The women were escorted to the table and seated before De Luca and Provenzano took their seats. One of the servants immediately poured a small amount of wine into De Luca's goblet. He swirled it around, inhaled the aroma, then tasted it.

"Ahh, *Il Chianti è eccellente. Lei può servirlo, Guido.* You may serve," he translated for the women.

"*Grazi,* Don De Luca," Guido replied. He poured Chianti into Rachel's glass, then Fancy's, then De Luca's, and finally Provenzano's glass.

"*Saluto,*" De Luca said, lifting his glass.

The others lifted their glasses as well.

"*Saluto!*" they responded.

They took a swallow, then De Luca lifted his glass again.

"To Nicholas Morello," De Luca said. *"Lui possa vagare attraverso inferno quardando per la sua testa."*

De Luca, Provenzano, and the Italian servants standing

around the table all laughed. When Provenzano saw the confused look in the faces of Rachel and Fancy, he interpreted for them.

"The Don said of Morello, 'May he wander through hell, looking for his head,'" Provenzano said. "It is a joke about someone we knew."

"Oh," Rachel said, not understanding the humor.

Guido returned to the table then, carrying an envelope.

"Don De Luca," Guido said. "Here is the money you asked for."

"Is the money all in federal bills? I don't want any local banknotes."

"*Sí,* Don De Luca. It is all in U.S. Government greenbacks," Guido said.

"*Grazi,*" De Luca said, taking the envelope. He pulled out some bills, counted them, then returned the bills to the envelope and stuck the envelope into his inside jacket pocket. He looked across the table at Rachel and smiled.

"Forgive me for the interruption, *signorina,*" he said. "But the cost of doing business with the police is quite high, and they insist upon federal bills. No local bank or promissory notes."

"I understand," Rachel said. "From time to time it has been necessary for Clarisse to do business with the police. They can be quite particular when it comes to how they wish to be paid."

"And sometimes they want to do business with us without paying at all," Fancy said.

"If your madam would agree to let me protect her operation, nobody would ever try and do business without paying again," De Luca said.

One of the servants brought out a serving dish and set it on the table.

"Ah, *la nostra cena,*" De Luca said as the servant removed the silver cover.

"Our supper," Provenzano interpreted.

A few moments after they began eating, Guido came again to the table, then leaned over to speak quietly to De Luca.

"Show him in," De Luca said. "Luigi, set an extra plate for the police commissioner."

"*Sí,* Don De Luca."

The police commissioner was escorted back to the garden then. He was tall, gray-haired, and had a mustache, but no beard. He was wearing a white suit with a brown silk vest. De Luca rose to speak to him.

"Signore Hennesy, how nice of you to join our celebration."

" 'Celebration'?"

"*Sí,* our *celebrazione di indipendenza.* I'm having an extra plate set for you."

"Thank you, no," the commissioner said. "I can't stay long."

"I will be very disappointed, Signore Hennesy, if you do not honor our independence celebration," De Luca said pointedly. "You are here for your money, I know. But surely you can take the time to have supper with friends and two beautiful women?"

Finally realizing that De Luca's invitation was more than an invitation, Hennesy acquiesced.

"Of course I will stay and have dinner with you, Don De Luca. And I thank you—very much—for your kind invitation."

"I am honored that you accepted."

"I have heard that Tangeleno may be looking to have a . . . what is that word you Italians use for revenge?"

"We are Sicilian," De Luca said. "And the word you are looking for is 'vendetta.' But do not worry yourself about Tangeleno. We can take care of ourselves."

"Perhaps that is true, but I'm sure you realize what difficulty a full-scale war between you and Tangeleno would cause. For all of us," Hennesy added pointedly.

De Luca laughed. "You mean you are afraid that if I am killed, your money will be cut off." De Luca reached for his inside pocket. "Well, don't worry about a thing. Tangeleno will not dare attack me. He knows I am too . . ." The sound of a gunshot interrupted De Luca's comment.

"Uhn!" De Luca grunted.

Rachel saw blood spurt onto the table, then she looked up in horror as De Luca put both his hands to his throat. His eyes were open wide in pain and surprise, and she saw his hands turning red with blood.

"It is Tangeleno!" Hennesy shouted. Pulling his pistol, he spun around, but the police commissioner went down before he could get off a shot, taking a hit in the chest by a shotgun blast.

The first few shots were followed immediately by a fusillade of gunfire as more than a dozen men suddenly burst into the garden, shooting pistols, rifles, and shotguns.

Nearly all of De Luca's men were armed, and they began firing back. Bullets and loads of buckshot whizzed through the air. Wine bottles burst, sending out showers of wine, food was hit, and pieces were scattered across the table.

The men screamed at each other, and even though it was in Italian, Rachel knew that they were shouting curses.

Rachel and Fancy were exchanging looks of terror when suddenly the front of Fancy's lavender dress turned red with blood as she was hit.

"Fancy!"

"Rachel?" Fancy said. She sounded more surprised than frightened. As Fancy called out Rachel's name, blood began oozing from her mouth. She went down.

"Fancy, oh my God, no!" Rachel cried as she started toward her.

"Rachel, get down!" Pietro Fanchetti shouted, suddenly appearing as if from nowhere. Pietro ran across the garden, firing at the invaders, roaring curses at them as he did so. When he reached Rachel, he shoved her hard, pushing her down to the ground.

Rachel lay where she fell, trying to block out the horror of what was going on. She looked up at Pietro and saw him take a hit from a load of buckshot that sent a shower of blood and brains bursting out the side of his head.

That blast slammed Pietro against the dining table, knocking it over. The table fell on Rachel and she felt a blow to her head.

After that, everything went dark.

Chapter 17

~

IT WAS DARK.

The soft cooing of the pigeons and the fluttering of their wings seeped into Rachel's consciousness.

She felt a little chilly and wished she had put the window down, but didn't want to get out of bed to do it. She reached for the sheet and pulled it up over her shoulders.

The sheet was wet and sticky. What was it? What had she spilled on her bed?

Rachel opened her eyes and saw the pigeons eating bread from the ground.

What was bread doing on the ground?

She turned her head and stared directly into the face of Fancy, who was staring back at her. Fancy's once-beautiful brown eyes were open, opaque, and sightless.

Suddenly Rachel realized where she was! She remembered, also, the screams, the shouts, the gunshots, and the blood.

"Oh my God!" she said in a quiet sob.

The sheet she had pulled over her shoulders was the tablecloth; the wet stickiness she had been feeling was blood. Recoiling in horror, she pushed the tablecloth away.

Rachel wanted more than anything in the world to scream, but she fought hard to hold it back. What if the people who did this were still here? Would they be coming for her now?

Rachel wasn't really hurt, except for a bump and a very tender spot on her head. She was lying under the table and had evidently been knocked out by it when it overturned. The fact that she was covered by the table—and unconscious—probably saved her life, because the shooters thought she was already dead.

Slowly and carefully, Rachel got to her feet, then looked around. She counted eight bodies, including Fancy, De Luca, Provenzano, Guido, Luigi, and Pietro. She realized then that Pietro, as much as the table, was responsible for her still being alive, because he had pushed her to the ground when the firing started.

If only there had been someone to do the same thing for Fancy.

"Oh, Fancy," she said. A lump came to her throat and tears filled her eyes. She crawled over to Fancy and then reached out to close her eyes.

"They're in the back," a voice said.

Someone was coming and for a moment Rachel was glad. She started to call out to them, then she checked the impulse. What if they were the same people who had done this? What if they were coming back to finish the job?

She had to get out of here!

Getting to her feet, Rachel moved quickly to the side of the garden where she managed to step behind a sculptured piece of shrubbery just before the visitors arrived.

Rachel peeked through the shrubbery and saw a golden

bubble of light as two men appeared around the corner of the house. One of the men was carrying a lighted lantern, the other was carrying a gun.

"The first thing we need to do is get the two women out of here," the one with the gun said. "When the police find De Luca and the others back here, the newspaper will just report that it was a bunch of Sicilians having it out with each other and they'll say good riddance. But if they find a couple of women among the dead, there will be hell to pay."

"The women were whores," the other man said. As they came closer, the light of the lantern enabled Rachel to get a good look at them. She recognized them both. One was Joe Tangeleno, the other was Sal Vizzini.

"I don't care if they're whores or not, they're women," Tangeleno said. "If it is discovered that we killed a couple of women, we're going to get a lot of bad reaction from the . . ." Tangeleno started, then he stopped in midsentence and pointed to one of the bodies. "What in the hell? Is that Hennesy, the police commissioner?"

"Yes," Vizzini said.

"*Madre di Dio!* You killed the police commissioner?" Tangeleno asked in an angry voice. "What the hell were you thinking of, Vizzini? Were you out of your mind?"

"What could we do, Don Tangeleno?" Vizzini asked defensively. "He happened to be here when we showed up. We couldn't just say, 'Sorry, my mistake.' Besides, the son of a bitch was being paid off by De Luca. He was one of De Luca's men, no different from Provenzano, or Guido, or Fanchetti, or any of them."

"Maybe so, but this isn't good," Tangeleno said, running his hand through his hair. "This isn't good at all. Once word gets out that we killed a police commissioner . . . the city will do whatever it takes to put us out of business. If they have to, they will form a militia to stop us."

"He was not an honest policeman," Vizzini said. "Hell, everybody knows that."

"Do you think that will matter to the people in town?"

"You know none of our people will talk. Everyone is sworn to the code of *omerta*."

"If the body is found here, no one will have to talk. The police aren't dumb. We have to get him out of here. Take him out when we get the two women out of here."

"What will we do with them?"

"Take them down to the river and dump them. The current will take the bodies out into the Gulf," Tangeleno said.

"All right," Vizzini agreed.

Tangeleno continued to walk through the bodies, looking down at them. He rolled De Luca's body over with his foot.

"Yes, here he is. The *bastardo* I was looking for," Tangeleno said in a snarling voice.

"Is that De Luca?" Vizzini asked.

"Yes." Tangeleno stared down at the body. "You killed my friend and sent his head to me. Now you are in hell."

Tangeleno put his thumb in his own eye, then jerked it away pointedly.

"Un occhio per un occhio!" he said with a sneer. "An eye for an eye."

"Don Tangeleno," Vizzini said. "One of them is missing."

"One of who is missing?"

"One of the women. There were two women here. Now there is only one."

"Are you sure there were two?"

"Yes."

"And you are sure they were both dead?"

"Yes," Vizzini said.

"So what are you saying, that a dead body just got up and

walked away? Because nobody would come here and remove just one body."

"I think she was dead," Vizzini said.

"You *think* she was dead?" Tangeleno said, his voice clearly showing his irritation.

"The last time I saw her she was lying right there." He pointed to where Rachel had been.

"Who was the woman? Do you know her name?"

"Yes, I know both their names. The colored girl"—he pointed to Fancy—"was called Fancy. I don't know if that was really her name."

"It doesn't make any difference what her name is, *stupido*. She is dead and she is here. What is the other woman's name? Is she colored too?"

"No, she's white. Her name is Rachel."

"What is her last name?"

Vizzini shook his head. "I don't think whores have last names."

"Of course whores have last names, *lei l'idiota!*" Tangeleno said angrily.

"I don't know her last name."

"If she is still alive she is very dangerous to us, because she is a witness," Tangeleno said. "Not only to this"—he took in all the bodies with a wave of his hand—"but she also saw us kill the police commissioner."

"That's not good," Vizzini said.

"You said she is a whore. Where does she whore?"

"Yes!" Vizzini said, hitting his hand into his fist. "That's where she is. She works at the House of the Evening Star. I'm sure that's where she went. She has no other place to go."

"We must find her."

"You want me to bring her to you?"

"No. I am going with you. We can't afford anymore mistakes."

"All right."

"Call Benito and Umberto back here now. Have them take away the police commissioner and the colored girl."

"Do you think the citizens of New Orleans are going to be upset over a dead colored whore?" Vizzini asked.

"Just get her out of here," Tangeleno said.

"All right."

Rachel continued to watch from her vantage point behind the shrubbery. Tangeleno stayed back while Vizzini left. Tangeleno walked over to De Luca's body and stared down at it.

"*Io piscio su Lei per Nick Morello, Lei il bastardo!* he said angrily. "I piss on you for Nick Morello."

Then, unbuttoning his pants, Tangeleno peed on De Luca's body.

Tangeleno was just rebuttoning his trousers when Vizzini showed up with Benito and Umberto. Vizzini pointed to Fancy and to the police commissioner.

"That one and that one," Vizzini said.

The two men made no response, but effortlessly scooped up the two bodies and draped them across their shoulders. Then all four men left.

Rachel remained behind the shrub for at least five more minutes, until she was completely satisfied that Tangeleno and Vizzini weren't coming back.

She had to get out of here. In fact, she had to get out of New Orleans. But how was she going to do that? She couldn't go back to the House of the Evening Star. They would be waiting for her there. On the other hand, if she didn't go back to her room, she would have no money, no clothes, no way to . . . wait a minute!

Rachel thought about the money De Luca had put into his jacket pocket. Was it still there? And if so, how much was there? Was there enough money to allow her to get out of New Orleans?

A nearly full moon provided enough light to allow her to pick her way through the carnage until she reached De Luca's body. Fortunately, Tangeleno had already turned him over. She was glad he had done that. It was going to be hard enough to look into his jacket pocket. It would have been even harder to actually touch him.

Steeling herself, Rachel knelt beside him and stared into his face. His face was still wet, and smelled of urine. One eye was half-closed, the other was fully open. There was a bullet hole in his neck and another in his left cheek. Both bullet holes were black and ugly-looking.

She opened his jacket and stuck her hand down into the inside pocket. Feeling the envelope, she pulled it out.

"Please let there be enough money to buy a railroad ticket out of here," she said aloud in a quiet prayer.

Rachel removed the money from the envelope, then gasped when she saw it. As De Luca said, the bills were all federal bills, which meant they were legal tender anywhere in America. And they were all one hundred dollar bills. She was absolutely certain there were at least twenty-five of them.

She was holding twenty-five hundred-dollar bills: $2,500!

For a moment she felt dizzy over her fantastic luck. She had wanted enough money to be able to get out of town, but she had no idea she would get this much money.

Then she felt guilty. She could justify taking enough money to escape. But how could she justify this?

Wait a minute. What was she thinking about? Who was she taking it from? De Luca was going to give it to the police officer, but neither of them had a use for it now. And she couldn't see letting it fall into the hands of the men who did all this.

Clutching the money, Rachel stood up. She adjusted her gown, then saw some blood on her dress. It was black in the moonlight and somehow that made it even more ghastly-looking than if it had been red.

She wished she could go back to the Evening Star to pack and change clothes, but that was impossible. Blood or no blood on her dress, she had to get out of town right now, but where would she go? What would she do?

"Louise!" Rachel said aloud. She would go west to see Louise. She could get a fresh start there.

Oh, if only this had happened yesterday, she thought. Then she could have left on the same boat that Mason Hawke left on. She would feel safe if she was traveling with him. She knew that he was just a piano player . . . but somehow she thought he was more than that.

Wait a minute. It's not too late. Trains travel much faster than riverboats. She could take a train north, upriver, then join the boat.

Straightening up her dress and combing her hair, she made herself as presentable as possible, then left.

Before going to the depot, Rachel stopped by the riverboat terminal to study the schedules of all the riverboats going north. It was just as she thought. It would be quite easy for her to overtake the *Delta Mist*. That would allow her to join Mason Hawke. He wasn't expecting her, of course, but she was sure that he would help her . . . for old times' sake—if for no other reason.

"One hundred dollars?" the railroad ticket agent asked in surprise. He studied the bill Rachel had given him.

"Yes, is there anything wrong? I was assured by the bank that this is a federal note and would be legal tender anywhere."

"No, there's nothing wrong. It is just that I don't see very many bills this large."

"I am going to be doing some traveling," Rachel said. "And I thought it might be easier to have my money converted into a few large bills."

"Very well, a ticket to Memphis," the ticket agent said. He

picked up a lead ink stamp and began stamping on the tickets. Then he handed the tickets to Rachel.

"Thank you."

"That'll be nine dollars," the ticket agent said. "You'll change trains in Jackson, Mississippi. I'll get a porter for your luggage."

"That's all right."

"It's no problem, madam. It's what they are here for."

"I . . . uh . . . don't have any luggage," Rachel admitted.

The ticket agent looked surprised. "You have no luggage?"

"No, I, uh, will be buying all new things when I get to Memphis."

The ticket agent looked at her as if he didn't believe her. Then he saw the blood on her dress.

Rachel saw that he was looking at the blood and, self-consciously, she put her hand over it.

"Are you all right, miss?"

Rachel laughed, nervously. "I had a nosebleed."

The blood was on her skirt.

"A nosebleed?"

"Yes," Rachel said pointedly. "It happens frequently. Do you know if the train is on time?" she asked, changing the subject.

"As far as I know, it is on time."

"Thank you."

Chapter 18

"YOU'VE GOT SOME NERVE COMING BACK HERE," Clarisse said to Vizzini when he and Tangeleno showed up at the House of the Evening Star. "Well, you are wasting your time. Evangeline doesn't want to see you anymore."

"I don't care anything about that bitch," Vizzini said. "Where is Rachel?"

"Rachel? If Evangeline won't see you, what makes you think that Rachel will? Anyway, Rachel has an engagement this evening."

"Get her," Vizzini said in a menacing voice.

"I can't get her. I told you, she isn't here. She is keeping an appointment elsewhere tonight."

"Where is her room?" Tangeleno said.

"It's upstairs."

"All the whores' rooms are upstairs," Tangeleno said, gruffly. "Which room is hers?"

"It's the first room on the right when you reach the top of the stairs, but I told you . . ."

Even as Clarisse was talking to them, Tangeleno and Vizzini pushed by her and started up the stairs, doing it so quickly that they forced a customer who was coming downstairs into the wall.

"Hey, who do you think . . ." the customer started to say, but Vizzini turned around quickly with a gun in his hand.

"You have something to say?" Vizzini asked.

"No no," the man replied quickly. "I don't have anything to say."

"I didn't think so."

When they reached Rachel's room, Tangeleno tried the door, but it was locked. Stepping back from the door, he kicked it hard, right beside the doorknob. The door popped open.

"Hey! What's going on out there?" a man's voice shouted from inside one of the rooms.

"Don't you worry about it," Vizzini said. Then he shouted down the hall for everyone to hear. "You men just stay in bed with your whores. If anybody sticks their head out into the hall, I'm going to blow it off!"

By now Clarisse was at the top of the stairs, having followed the two of them up.

"Why did you do that? I told you she wasn't here," Clarisse said angrily. She pointed to the door. "Somebody is going to have to pay for that door."

Tangeleno pulled some money from his pocket and handed it to Clarisse. "Will this cover it?" he asked.

Clarisse looked at the money. There were several twenty-dollar bills.

"Yes," she said. "Yes, I believe this will cover it."

"Light the lantern," Tangeleno said. "Let's have a look around."

Vizzini lit the lantern that sat on the dresser in Rachel's room.

"What is all this about?" Clarisse asked. "What are you doing in Rachel's room? What are you looking for?"

"What is Rachel's last name?" Tangeleno asked.

"I don't know."

"What do you mean you don't know? She works here, doesn't she? Isn't she one of your girls? How long has she been here?"

"Not very long," Clarisse said. She was growing more cautious and circumspect with her answers now, because she didn't know what all this was about.

"I know she's been here over a year," Vizzini said as he looked through things on her dresser. "Because I have been seeing her here for that long."

"She's been here for over a year and you don't know her last name?" Tangeleno asked.

"I never ask any of my girls for their last name," Clarisse replied. "Most of them only stay for a short while, then they go on to other lives. When they do that, they don't like for their past to catch up with them."

"Don Tangeleno, look at this," Vizzini said, taking a packet of letters from a little rosewood box. He handed the packet of letters to Tangeleno.

"What are you doing? Those are Rachel's private letters!" Clarisse said, reaching for them. "You have no right to look at . . ."

Clarisse's proetest was cut off when Tangeleno brought the back of his hand across her cheek, driving her back onto Rachel's bed. Clarisse sat down, hard, and held her hand to a cheek that was already beginning to show a bruise.

"Who is Louise Smalley?" Tangeleno asked as he looked at the letters.

Clarisse didn't answer. Instead, she sat on the edge of the bed, staring at the two men with eyes that showed not only her anger but were now welling with tears.

Tangeleno drew his hand back as if ready to hit her again. "I asked you a question," he said. "Who is Louise?"

"Louise used to work here," Clarisse answered in a frightened voice. "She was Rachel's friend."

Tangeleno looked through all the letters. "What is this? No letters from her family?"

"The only family Rachel has is Fancy."

"Fancy?" Vizzini asked. "What do you mean, she is the only family?"

"Fancy is Rachel's sister. But Fancy isn't here either."

"What are you trying to tell me?" Vizzini asked. "Fancy is colored."

"She is only half-colored," Clarisse said. "She and Rachel shared the same father."

Vizzini laughed out loud. "Well, I'll be damned. So her daddy liked the ladies who had a touch of the brush, did he?"

"Fancy is her only blood relative, but I like to think that we are all her family here. And if she is in trouble, any one of us would do whatever we can to help her."

"Anyone would do anything to help her?" Tangeleno asked. He held up the letters. "How about this woman? Do you think she would also do anything to help Rachel?"

"Yes, of course she would. Louise is married now, but I do believe she would help if she were needed. We are all very close here. Now please tell me what this is all about."

"Nothing," Tangeleno said, putting the letter with the latest date into his pocket. "Nothing at all. I'm sorry we bothered you. Come on, Vizzini. Let's go."

"Where are we going?" Vizzini asked.

"If you were going to go to Kansas, how would you go?"

"By train."

"Where do you find trains?"

Vizzini smiled. "At the railroad station," he said.

Chapter 19

THE TICKET AGENT LOOKED UP WITH SOME CU-
riosity and a little concern as the two approached his window.

"Yes, gentlemen, what can I do for you?" he asked.

"We're looking for a woman," Vizzini replied. "We think
that she may have bought a ticket from you."

"A lot of ladies buy railroad tickets."

"We are only interested in one, and she would have bought
it earlier this evening. We want to know when she left and
where she is going."

"I'm sorry, but unless you are with the police, I don't think
I could answer such a question."

"Mister, if you know what is good for you, you will . . ."
Vizzini started, but Tangeleno held up his hand, interrupting
him in midsentence.

"You might say we are working with the police," Tangeleno said.

"Do you have some sort of identification?" the ticket agent
asked.

"Yes, as a matter of fact, we do," Tangeleno replied, handing the ticket agent a twenty-dollar bill.

The agent took the twenty-dollar bill, examined it for a moment to make certain that it was legitimate, then folded it and put it away. He smiled at Tangeleno and Vizzini. "Yes," he said. "I think this is all the identification I will need. But let's step away from the ticket window, shall we?"

"Why?"

"One can't be too careful," the ticket agent said as he walked down to the far end of the counter. Tangeleno and Vizzini walked with him, keeping the counter between them.

"I must say that, earlier tonight, there was a woman who bought a ticket from me under most curious conditions. She was a very pretty young woman, about five feet four inches tall."

"That sounds like half the women in New Orleans," Vizzini said. "What makes you remember this one?"

"Three things. First, she paid for her ticket with a one hundred dollar bill. And second, she had no luggage."

"You said three things," Vizzini said.

"Oh yes. The third thing is: She had blood on her dress. She said it was from a nosebleed, but I didn't believe her."

"What color was the dress?"

"I believe it was yellow," the agent answered.

"Ticket agent, I would like a railroad ticket please," a man called from the window.

"Excuse me for a moment," the ticket agent said. The ticket agent walked back down to the window, far enough away to be out of earshot of Tangeleno and Vizzini.

"That's Rachel," Vizzini said. "It has to be. She was wearing a yellow dress, and I don't see how she could not have gotten blood on it."

"But the agent said she paid for her ticket with a one hundred dollar bill. Where did she get such money?"

"Maybe De Luca paid her to come to his party," Vizzini suggested.

"Why would he pay a whore one hundred dollars when he could get her for five dollars?"

"I don't know. But if he didn't pay her, where did she get the money?"

"Hennesy," Tangeleno said.

"Hennesy?"

"You said he was there, didn't you? De Luca was paying him off. Did you find any money?"

"We didn't look," Tangeleno admitted.

"That's where she got the money," Tangeleno said.

"I'm sorry, Don, I should have looked for the money.

To Vizzini's surprise, Tangeleno smiled. "No," he said. He chuckled. "This is working out very well."

"What do you mean?"

"We didn't think she had enough money to go where she wanted to go and we had no idea where she would wind up. But now that she does have money, we know exactly where she is going. She's going to Bellefont, Kansas."

"But the ticket agent said she only bought a ticket to Memphis."

"I know. But I think that was just to throw us off."

"I'm sorry for the interruption, gentlemen," the ticket agent said, returning from the transaction at the window. "Is there anything else I can help you with?"

"Yes. If this woman was going to Bellefont, Kansas, where would she change trains?"

"Well, she isn't going to Bellefont," the ticket agent said. "I sold her tickets only as far as Memphis."

"Yes, I know, but it may be that she did that just to throw off the police. If she was going to Bellefont, where would she go from Memphis?"

"Oh well, in that case, she would have to continue on up to St. Louis and take the train west from there," the ticket agent said. "But if that is so, why didn't she just buy a ticket all the way to St. Louis? It would have been cheaper to buy it all together, rather than buy it as a separate ticket."

"Who knows the workings of a criminal mind?" Tangeleno asked.

"Yes, who indeed," the ticket agent replied.

"What do we do now?" Vizzini asked as they left the station.

"I don't know about you, but I'm going home and going to bed," Tangeleno said. "It has been a long night."

"But Rachel?"

"Rachel is on the train, headed for Memphis. We can't do anything about her until she gets there."

"How? If the train has already left, we can't beat it to Memphis."

Tangeleno smiled. "We can't . . . but a telegram can."

The sign on the front of the store on West Capitol Street in Jackson, Mississippi, read: LADIES' CLOTHING AND MILLINERY GOODS.

"Yes, may I help you?" a woman asked, coming up to the counter when Rachel entered.

"I do hope so," Rachel replied. "I am on my way to Memphis. But when I changed trains here in Jackson, my luggage was sent, by mistake, to Montgomery, Alabama. I simply must have some clothes if I am to continue my journey. I hope you have some ready-made clothes that I could buy."

"Oh, you are in luck, my dear," the store clerk said. "I have several beautiful dresses that our own seamstresses have made. I'm sure we can get you outfitted quite nicely."

One hour later Rachel left the store wearing a new dress and carrying a portmanteau filled with the rest of her wardrobe. Hailing a hack, she had the driver take her to the Illinois Central Railroad Station. There, she exchanged her Memphis ticket for one that would take her to Cairo, Illinois.

* * *

As Tangeleno sat on his patio, having breakfast, one of his servants brought a man back to see him. The man wore a sweeping mustache and a bowler hat, and he took his hat off and made a sweeping bow as he was introduced.

"*I miei rispetti a Lei, Padrino,*" the man said. "I kiss your ring."

Tangeleno, who was sitting at the breakfast table, dabbed at his mouth with a linen, then held his ring out to allow the man to kiss it.

"What is your name?" Tangeleno asked.

"*Il mio nome è* Giovanni Giordano," the man replied. "I am a baker. My shop is at 1124 Bourbon Street. I have brought you some cannolis." He picked up a package, wrapped in cheesecloth, and held it toward Tangeleno. Tangeleno nodded at his servant, and the servant took it.

"*Grazie.* What can I do for you, Signore Giordano?"

"I did not tell the police," Giordano said.

Tangeleno squinted his eyes. "You did not tell the police what?" he asked.

"I did not tell them about the *pianista* who plays piano at the whorehouse."

"Signore Giordano, I still don't know what you are talking about."

"It was last week," Giordano said. "I was working late when I saw it." As Giordano began telling the story of witnessing a gun battle in the empty lot next to his bakery, it was clear that he was reliving the trauma of what he had witnessed.

"The police questioned me," Giordano said after he finished telling his story to Tangeleno. "But I said nothing. *Omerta, omerta.*" He put his finger to his lips.

"Then I learned that the men the whorehouse piano player killed were your men, Don Tangeleno. And because they were your men and because of my great respect for you, I have come to tell you."

Tangeleno had listened incredulously to the entire story. It seemed improbable that one man could kill three of his best men in such a way. It seemed impossible that the one man who did it would be a whorehouse piano player.

And yet, even as he was weighing the credulity, Tangeleno knew he believed the story. He believed the story because there was no way this baker would know that he had sent his men after the piano player.

"My friend," Tangeleno said, putting his hand on Giordano's shoulder. "You have done right in coming to me like this. You have done me a great favor. What can I do for you?"

"There is a colored woman in the 800 block of Rampart Street," Tangeleno said. "She is making bread and pastries. It is all right if she makes it for her own kind, but she is making Italian bread and pastries. She is not as good as I am, she does not know all the secrets of the old country. And because she does not use the best ingredients, she sells for less money than I can sell for. She is hurting my business."

"It is not good that a colored woman bakes for Italians. I will go and talk to her," Tangeleno promised. "I will make her listen to reason."

"*Grazie, Padrino,*" Giordano said, again kissing Tangeleno's ring. "*Grazie.*"

That evening, as Tangeleno was having his supper, Vizzini stepped into the dining room. Tangeleno had just lifted a forkful of spaghetti to his mouth and he sucked in all the noodles before he spoke.

"What do you have to tell me?" Tangeleno asked.

"The colored woman that Giordano spoke about will not be baking any more bread for Italians. I spoke to her, and I got her to listen to reason."

"Good, good," Tangeleno said.

"Also, I have found out some very interesting things," Vizzini said.

"Such as?"

"The man who played the piano at the whorehouse is named Mason Hawke."

"What do you mean, 'the man who *played* the piano'?"

"He is no longer there, Don Tangeleno. He has left New Orleans."

"Where did he go?"

"He took a job on the riverboat *Delta Mist* and is on his way to St. Louis."

"St. Louis?" Tangeleno picked up a napkin and dabbed at his lips. "So, the man who played the piano in the same house where the whore Rachel worked is going to St. Louis."

"It is even more interesting, Don Tangeleno," Vizzini said. "I have heard that the whore and this man Hawke knew each other from before. They were friends before the American Civil War."

"When did the boat leave New Orleans?" Tangeleno asked.

"It left yesterday morning."

"And the whore left last night."

"Yes."

Tangeleno smiled. "Now we know why she didn't buy a ticket all the way to St. Louis. She plans to join the boat in Memphis."

"Don Tangeleno, I think there is something else you should know about this piano player," Vizzini said. "This telegram came from Steffani Bellini in Denver. He held it out.

"Read it," Tangeleno said.

Vizzini cleared his throat and began reading. "'Understand you have had run-in with Mason Hawke Stop You should know that he is one of the deadliest gunmen in the

West Stop I do not know what he is doing in New Orleans, but do not take him lightly Stop.' "

"So," Tangeleno said. "It would appear that we had a wolf in sheep's clothing."

"*Sí*, Don Tangeleno."

"Vizzini, send telegrams to Memphis and to St. Louis. I want the piano player and the whore dead, and I will pay five thousand dollars to whoever does it."

"I will send the telegrams," Vizzini said.

"And just to be certain that the job is done, you and I will go to this place in Kansas where the whore is going."

"You want *me* to go to Bellefont with you?"

"Yes. You are *il mio tenente fidato*, my trusted lieutenant. If all others fail me, I know you will succeed. And when we have killed them both, I will give you your own city."

"I thank you for your confidence, Don Tangeleno," Vizzini said with a proud smile.

Chapter 20

IT WAS AN ALL-NIGHT TRIP FROM JACKSON TO
Memphis, and Rachel woke up the next morning, just as the
train was backing into the station. The sound of steel wheels
rolling on steel tracks, as well as the puffing of the steam engine, echoed back from the roof that stretched overhead.

As this train would be going on to Cairo, she did not have
to detrain, so she lay there, enjoying the comforting and almost guilty sensation of being able to remain in bed while
others were having to move about.

She had just about dozed off again when she heard something that alerted her.

"Is your name Rachel?"

The question was asked by a man, and, very carefully,
Rachel peeked through the still-closed curtains that shut off
her upper berth. She saw two men standing in the aisle, about
three-quarters of the way toward the far end of the car.

"No, my name is not Rachel," a woman answered. The
woman was blonde, and about Rachel's age.

"I beg your pardon for disturbing you, ma'am," the man
who asked the question said.

The two men passed on through the car, but, as the woman sitting in the seat was the only woman who was close to her age and description, they didn't ask anyone else.

"What's her last name?" one of the men asked.

"I don't know. The telegram from Tangeleno didn't say."

Rachel's blood ran cold when she heard Tangeleno's name.

Even as the first man was answering the question, he jerked open one of the closed curtains.

"Hey! This berth is taken!" a man's voice said from behind the curtains.

"Sorry."

Rachel was terrified! How did Tangeleno know she was on this train?

"Maybe she's already off the train," one of the men said.

"Could be, but I'm not going to take any chances. Tangeleno's not a man you want to disappoint."

Rachel heard another curtain jerked open. "This one is empty."

They were coming here!

Rachel moved to the inside of her bed, where it attached to the side of the car. Reaching back to the edge, she pulled back, causing the bed to pivot up, then snap closed. It was tight and dark inside. She heard the curtains open.

"She's not here. This bed has already been folded up."

"How come the curtains are closed?"

"I don't know, but she's not here."

"If she's already off the train, we better get out there and find her."

"Yeah."

Rachel remained very quiet for a long time. Not until the train began moving again, did she start knocking on the bunk and calling out.

"Is someone in there?" a man's voice called.

"Yes! I'm in here!"

She heard the key being put into the keyhole, then, mercifully, the bunk was pulled down. She found herself looking directly into the face of a black porter.

"Lord have mercy, miss, how'd you get yourself wound up in such a fix?" the porter asked.

"I don't know," Rachel said. "I just turned over against the inside of the bed and it pivoted up."

"Well, how long you been in there?"

"Since we arrived in Memphis."

"If that don't beat all. I'm terrible sorry, miss," the porter said. "I'll take a good look at it to see that it don't happen again."

"Thank you."

As the train approached Caruthersville, Missouri, Rachel decided to get off. Somehow the two men who were looking for her in Memphis had known that she was on that train. The only way they could have possibly known was to have traced her through the ticket agent who sold her the original ticket, back in New Orleans.

Since they did not find her in Memphis, what would keep them from learning that she had bought a ticket to Cairo?

The answer was: Nothing could prevent them from making that discovery. But if she arbitrarily decided to leave the train in Caruthersville, who would know? She had told nobody of this decision. She had not even come to this decision until just before the train reached Caruthersville.

Caruthersville was a river port, and the train was now well ahead of the *Delta Mist*. All she would have to do is wait here for a few days, then board the boat when it made its port call.

"I beg your pardon?" the conductor asked when she told him she wished to get off.

"I want to get off here," she said again.

"I'm not authorized to give you a refund for the unused portion of your ticket," the conductor said.

"I don't want a refund. I'll use it to complete my trip later," Rachel said. She told him the lie, because she believed that the fewer people who knew her real plans, the safer she would be. "It's just that I would like to visit here for a while."

"I wish you had told us that earlier, miss. It is going to be difficult to locate your luggage."

"I'm sorry for the inconvenience."

Within a few minutes of the conversation, the train began slowing as it approached the depot. Rachel stepped down onto the wooden depot platform and waited as the conductor went up to the baggage car to arrange for her luggage. Despite his protestations, her suitcase was produced quickly, and she stood there with it beside her as the engineer blew two long whistles, then started forward.

It was Rachel's plan to remain as inconspicuous as she possibly could until it was time for her to board the riverboat. If nobody knew she was here, there would be no way of tracing her.

The problem with her plan, she learned as soon as the train pulled away from the station, was that Caruthersville was a very tiny town. And as an attractive single woman, she was guaranteed to attract attention.

"What brings you to our little town, Miss Smith?" the hotel clerk asked reading the name Rachel had used for her registration.

"I'm on my way to St. Louis to take a job as a schoolteacher," Rachel replied.

The clerk looked surprised. "I don't understand," he said. "You just got off a train that is going to St. Louis."

Rachel started to ask how he knew she had just left the

train, but knew the answer without having to ask the question. The hotel clerk knew because everyone in town knew. No doubt, everyone in town knew what she was wearing also, as well as how tall she was, and the color of her hair and eyes.

"The motion of the train was making me ill," Rachel said. "I thought, perhaps, the slower and more leisurely pace of a riverboat would be less disturbing."

"Yes, riding on a train can make one sick," the clerk agreed. "I have been sick a few times myself."

Rachel took the key from the clerk, went upstairs to her room, and settled in for the two-day stay. She wondered how she was going to keep herself occupied during her stay, then she thought of Louise. This would be the perfect opportunity to send a telegram, because she would have the time to wait for Louise's reply.

The Western Union office was in the depot, and as she walked there, she met at least half a dozen other pedestrians and was greeted as Miss Smith by all of them. Even the telegrapher knew the name she had registered by.

"Hello, Miss Smith," he said. "I hope you are enjoying Caruthersville."

"Yes, it's quite a lovely town. I would like to send a telegram."

"Yes, ma'am," the telegrapher said. He picked up a tablet and pencil. "Who is your message to?"

"It is to Mrs. Louise Smalley in Bellefont, Kansas," Rachel said. " 'Is Queen of Hearts still for sale?' "

"Is that it?" the telegrapher asked.

"Sign it 'Rachel'."

"All right," the telegrapher said. He counted the words. "That will be four bits."

Rachel gave him a dollar bill, then received fifty cents in

change. "How long will it be before I receive an answer?" she asked.

"Well, that's pretty much up to Mrs. Smalley. I expect she'll have this message in no more'n half an hour from now."

"Oh, isn't this the most wonderful invention?" Rachel asked.

"Yes, ma'am, it is."

As Rachel returned to the hotel, though, she remembered that the men who had come on the train in Memphis had been alerted to her presence by telegram. The same telegraph service she was so enthused about was making it possible for Tangeleno to continue his hunt for her.

One hour later Rachel was lying on the bed in her room when she was surprised—and a little frightened—to hear a knock on her door. She sat up but said nothing. Had they traced her here already?

"Miss Smith?"

Smith? Rachel breathed a little easier. Nobody but the residents of this town would call her Smith.

"Yes?" Rachel answered.

"I have a telegram for you," the voice called from the other side of the door. It was obviously the voice of a young boy.

Rachel opened the door and saw a red-haired, freckle-faced youth of about fourteen. She gave him a dime.

"Thank you!" the boy said, grinning broadly at the tip.

Closing the door, Rachel walked back into her room and sat on the bed before she opened the telegram. She breathed a quick prayer that the response would be what she wanted.

Yes Stop Come as Soon as You Can Stop Louise

Rachel's spirits were greatly buoyed by the telegram. Until now, she had been unsure of what she was going to do, other than escape Tangeleno. But with the news that the Queen of Hearts was still for sale, and with well over two thousand dollars in cash, she felt a sense of direction in her life for the first time since she had left Georgia.

Chapter 21

❦

THE LIGHTS OF CARUTHERSVILLE, MISSOURI, SLIPPED behind the riverboat as it beat its way upriver on the way to St. Louis.

In the Grand Salon, Mason Hawke was playing Chopin's Piano Concerto Number 2 in F Minor to an audience that was more attentive—and much quieter—than his usual saloon audience. It had been eight days since Hawke signed on to the *Delta Mist* in New Orleans, and he had been providing music for the passengers nightly ever since.

When he finished the piece, he was rewarded with a generous applause, to which he stood and made acknowledgment with a small graceful bow.

With his last set completed, Hawke slid the bench under the piano and decided to take a break.

"Beautiful music, sir," someone called to him.

"Thanks," Hawke replied.

"That was lovely, Mr. Hawke, truly lovely," an elderly woman said.

"I appreciate your compliment, ma'am," Hawke said. He picked his way through the crowd, then pushed through the double doors and went out on deck to the refreshing coolness of the night air.

Hawke walked back to the stern of the boat and stood there for just a moment. As the boat progressed upriver, it left a wake of frothy foam behind the rapidly rolling giant wheel. The wake gleamed white under the moon that hung full and silver in the night sky.

As Hawke looked at the wake, he had a sudden and irrational thought. What if, like this boat, his life left a wake? And what if he could find a way to follow that wake fast enough—and far enough—to go back in time, to visit earlier portions of his life?

Would he really want to do that? There were times in his life that he really would like to visit; growing up on a plantation in Georgia, wrestling, fishing, and hunting with his brother. He would like to revisit his concert tour in Europe, just before the war began.

There was nothing about the war that he would revisit, but so much a part of him was that war, that it was always, just on the other side of memory. There was never rhyme nor reason to those memories, nor were any specific memories ever summoned. They just arrived, like the one that was pushing its way into his thoughts now.

The Yankees had come in by train the night before, a new regiment recently raised in Massachusetts. Not one of the soldiers, who were still wearing shiny new blue uniforms, had ever heard a shot fired in anger. They made camp, pitching their tents in neat, squared-off rows, as if they were back in Massachusetts, rather than in Northern Georgia. Laughing and talking loudly, they built fires, cooked their supper, then played guitars and banjos before going to bed that night.

After their father was killed, Mason Hawke's brother, Major Gordon Hawke, took command of "Hawke's Regiment."

In that capacity, Gordon called his men to a halt about three miles away from the Yankee camp. It was his belief that the best time to strike would be at dawn, so he had his men make a cold camp and sleep on the ground without even pitching a tent. The men didn't complain about eating hardtack and drinking water, but those who smoked were a little put out about not being able to light up.

"Captain," one of the men said to Mason Hawke. "Why don't you talk to your brother and see if he'll let us smoke?"

"Think about it, Tommy," Hawke said. "What would we accomplish by not having fires to cook food or make coffee if you're going to give away our position by smoking?"

"Oh yeah," Tommy said. "Yeah, I guess you're right."

If the men didn't like it, they at least understood the validity of it, so no one violated orders that night.

At dawn, Gordon divided his men into two groups. He gave Mason command of half the regiment and sent him around with instructions to attack the Yankee camp from the north. Gordon kept one group back to enter from the east.

It took half an hour for Mason to get his men into position, but he got there just as the sun was peeking up over the eastern horizon. Then, as had been arranged, he fired two shots into the air. His shots were answered by three shots, which was the prearranged signal to begin the attack.

"Let's go!" Hawke shouted and, drawing their pistols, he and his men rode at a gallop into the Yankee camp, firing into the air and through the canvas of the tents.

Several of the Yankee soldiers, many of them still wearing the long-handles they had slept in, ran out into the camp street to see what was going on. Then, shocked to see that they were actually under attack, they turned and ran back into the tents. A few of the soldiers came out with weapons in their hands, though for the most part the weapons weren't yet charged.

For nearly all of them, that proved to be a fatal mistake. They were cut down where they stood.

The two groups of riders met in the middle of the Yankee camp, laughing, shouting, and still firing into the air.

"All right, Yankees!" Gordon Hawke shouted out loud. "Turn out! Turn out of your tents so we can see you!"

When no one showed up, Gordon nodded at his sergeant, and his sergeant lit a torch, then tossed it into a stack of small wooden kegs.

"No! That's gunpowder!" one of the Yankees shouted and everyone scattered. The powder went up with a great roar, and when the smoke settled, there were nearly a dozen bodies lying around, including the body of Mason's brother, Major Gordon Hawke.

Chapter 22

⁓ ⁓

IN AN EFFORT TO BLOT THAT UNPLEASANT MEMory from his mind, Hawke removed a cheroot, lit it, then stepped over to the railing and looked out toward the Missouri side. The riverbank was solidly covered with trees—Cyprus, oak, elm—a dark growth that bespoke of the swampy forest behind.

"I was wondering if I would ever get the opportunity to talk to you alone," a woman's soft, well-modulated, and familiar voice said from the shadows behind Hawke.

Hawke toward the sound.

A woman stepped out of the shadows. As she came closer, Hawke could see her features, not only by moon glow, but by the gleam of a running lantern that hung from one of the pillars that supported the upper deck. She was wearing a white silk dress, cut daringly low. The dress shimmered in the moonlight.

"Rachel!" Hawke said, shocked at seeing her on the boat.

"Hello, Mason."

"What are you doing here? How did you get here? I thought you were back in New Orleans."

"Are you displeased?"

"What? No no, of course not. I just didn't expect to find you here."

Rachel smiled at Hawke. "You didn't expect to see me in a place like the Evening Star either, did you?" she asked. "That's why you didn't recognize me."

"Recognize you?"

Rachel sighed. "You really don't remember me, do you, Mason? I kept telling myself that maybe you did recognize me, but just didn't want to mention it."

"Rachel, I don't know what you are talking about. Are you saying that we met before the Evening Star?"

"Yes."

"I find that hard to believe. I rarely forget a beautiful woman."

"Why, Mason Hawke. What a lovely compliment," Rachel said. She laughed, her laughter sounding like the gentle playing of wind chimes.

"Well, I can't really hold it against you," she continued. "So much has happened since then. But I remember vividly the last time we met. My father held a party for your father's regiment. You were so handsome in your gray and gold uniform. I was very much in love with you then . . . though, of course, I was too shy to let you know."

"Your father held a party for the regiment? Are you talking about Charles Brubaker?"

"Yes."

Hawke got a confused look on his face. "I don't remember . . ."

"I don't really expect you to remember me," she said. "I was only twelve years old then. And although I am Rachel Brubaker, most people knew me then as Angel." She laughed. "That was my father's nickname for me, and I assure you, it had nothing to do with my behavior."

"Angel? Yes, I do remember you now." Hawke chuckled. "Wait a minute, aren't you the little girl who let the mouse go on the dance floor that night? It caused a panic among all the girls, as I recall . . . they ran around screaming, somebody knocked over the punch bowl, another crashed through the window."

"I'm the guilty party," Rachel admitted with a laugh. "I was upset because my father said I was too young to attend the dance. I wanted some reaction, but I got more than I bargained for."

Hawke laughed with her.

"I knew, from the moment you sat down to play the piano at the Evening Star, that you were the same person I remembered. You haven't lost any of your skill or talent, I see."

Hawke lifted his hand. "Oh, I'm going to have to differ with you there. I've lost a lot of my skill, I'm afraid. It's impossible to maintain skill if you are never challenged, and none of the many jobs I've held over the last several years have been particularly challenging."

"But you are still playing the piano, and from what I've heard for the last couple of months, you are playing it beautifully. I never asked you while you were there . . . in fact, it would have been inappropriate. But how did you wind up playing at a whorehouse in New Orleans?"

"Before I came to New Orleans, I was playing at a saloon in Nebraska for a woman named Callie."

"Callie? Big Callie?" Rachel asked.

"Yes, did you know her?"

"I know who she was. She was Clarisse's sister. Clarisse used to talk about her. But she was killed, I believe. Wait a minute, were you there when she was killed?"

"Yes."

"I didn't know that. Clarisse never talked about it that much. I think it was too hard for her to talk about. So you knew Big Callie. Was she anything like Clarisse?"

"They were both good women to work for," Hawke said. "That's why, when Big Callie was killed, I decided to come to New Orleans, as my own type of memorial to her."

"Where else have you been?"

"I've been everywhere in general, nowhere in particular," Hawke said. "I've been in Wyoming, Texas, Arizona, Colorado, Kansas, Nebraska . . ."

"Kansas?" she asked.

Hawke nodded. "Yes, I've played in Kansas."

"Do you know Bellefont?"

"I know Bellefont. I've never played there, but I have passed through. It's a rough town."

"That's where I'm going," Rachel said.

Hawke laughed. "I've got news for you, Rachel. You won't get there by riverboat."

Rachel laughed as well.

"I know. I took a train to Caruthersville, Missouri, then transferred to the boat."

"Why didn't you take the train directly to Bellefont? It would have been a lot faster."

"The reason I came aboard at Caruthersville was because I knew you were on the boat."

"Hmm. Should I be flattered or concerned?"

"How would you like to play the piano for me in Bellefont?"

"Well, I don't know. Will you have a place for me to play?"

"Yes. I'm going to Bellefont to buy a gambling house called the Queen of Hearts," Rachel said. "And it's not just any gambling house. I'm told it is the nicest one in town. When I start the business, I would like for you to play the piano for me."

"I appreciate the offer, Rachel, but I've got a job. I'm playing piano on this riverboat."

"Yes, but you aren't going to stay with this boat. You know you aren't."

"I don't stay anywhere very long."

"I gathered that. But I would be grateful for whatever time you did stay. You see, it's my theory that music, particularly beautiful music, has a calming effect and helps in keeping an orderly house."

"I don't know," Hawke said.

"You don't know that music has a calming effect?"

"Oh, I agree with that. I just don't know if I want to work for you."

Rachel looked hurt. "Why not? I know you have worked for women. You worked for Big Callie and you worked for Clarisse."

"That's different."

"What is different? I thought we had already established the fact that I'm not the twelve-year-old anymore."

"It's not that."

"What is it, then?"

Hawke turned away from her and leaned on the boat railing, looking out across the dark shimmering water toward the shore. A large crane stood on one leg in the shallow water near the shore, its white feathers nearly luminous in the full moon.

"You say you want me there so that my music will have a calming effect," he said.

"Yes."

"Somehow . . . despite my music, I don't seem to have a very calming effect on people. In fact, it's quite the opposite."

"Maybe that's another reason I want you to work for me," Rachel said.

"What do you mean? You want me to work because I *don't* have a calming effect on people?"

"No. I want you to work for me because whatever happens, I know you will be able to handle it. One of the things I remember about you from my youth—you might even say that it is one of the things that I most admired about you—was that you didn't let anyone push you around. Some of the boys seemed to think that you were a sissy for taking piano lessons, but if they said it to you, they only said it once."

"How do you know that?"

"Oh, word got around. Maybe that's one of the reasons I want to hire you now. As you said, Bellefont is a rough town."

Hawke flipped his cheroot into the river and followed the arc of the tiny red glow until the water snuffed it out. He turned back toward Rachel. "How in the world did you wind up . . ." he let the sentence hang.

"A whore?" she asked.

Hawke sighed. "Yeah," he said. He held up his hand. "And believe me, I'm not passing judgment on you. Lord knows, I'm the last one qualified to pass judgment on anyone."

"It's a long story," Rachel said. "I guess it comes as quite a shock to you that a genteel, plantation-raised Georgia girl would wind up in a whorehouse in New Orleans. And now that same genteel girl is going to a town like Bellefont to buy a gambling house."

Hawke chuckled. "Well no, what *is* a shock to me is that the girl who let a mouse loose on the dance floor became a genteel, plantation-raised Georgia girl."

"Mason, that's awful!" Rachel said, laughing and hitting him on the shoulder. "You have a cruel streak in you," she teased.

"I'm cruel? I'm not the one who turned the mouse loose."

"You haven't answered my question yet. Will you come work for me? I can pay you well."

"How well is 'well'?"

"I can pay you one of two ways," she said. "I can either pay you a straight salary, an amount that we can agree upon mutually, or I can give you a cut of the take. It's your choice."

Hawke stared at Rachel for a long moment, studying the

expression on her face. Unable to meet his intense gaze, Rachel broke off eye contact.

"There's something you aren't telling me, isn't there?"

"Lord, Mason, what could I possibly be holding back from you?" Rachel asked. "You saw me as a whore, I'm buying a gambling house. What could I possibly be holding back from you?"

"I don't know," Mason said. "But I think you had better tell me now."

Rachel sighed. "What I really want is for you to protect me."

"Protect you from what?"

"Do you know who the Mafia is?"

Hawke recalled his run-in with the three shooters in the dark on Dauphine Street.

"Are you talking about that bunch of Italians back in New Orleans? What were some of the names? Tangeleno was one, I think. And De Luci."

"De Luca," Rachel corrected. "Yes, that's who I'm talking about. Well, not De Luca. He's dead. That's why I'm running."

"You're running because De Luca is dead? You didn't kill him, did you?"

"No. But I saw him killed, and the people who killed him know that I saw it. That's why I'm running."

"They are an evil bunch, all right, but you're not in New Orleans anymore, so I don't see how they can hurt you now."

"Believe me, they aren't just in New Orleans," Rachel said. "They have people everywhere. Tangeleno telegraphed ahead to Memphis and a couple of them came on to the train in Memphis to get me."

"I take it that Tangeleno was the killer."

"Tangeleno, Vizzini, and several others."

"How did you happen to see this?"

"I was at De Luca's party when Tangeleno's men came into the backyard with guns. They started killing and they didn't stop until everyone was dead. Or, at least, they *thought* everyone was dead. I wound up under a table and some bodies, so they didn't realize that I wasn't dead." Rachel paused for a moment and Hawke saw tears glistening in her eyes. "They killed Fancy, Mason."

"For a little Georgia girl who once let a mouse loose on a dance floor, you have gotten yourself into a pickle, haven't you, Rachel Brubaker?"

Rachel nodded as she wiped away her tears. "I fear that I have," she said. "So now you can see why I would like to have you around."

"All right," Hawke agreed.

"You mean, you will come?"

"Sure, why not? One place is as good as another."

"Oh, thank you! Thank you!" Rachel said as, spontaneously, she leaned forward to kiss him.

Hawke was surprised by her unexpected action, and before he could respond she had already pulled back. "Bellefont, here we come!" she said with a happy smile. "I'll get us train tickets as soon as we get to St. Louis."

Hawke went back into the salon. Most of the passengers were engaged in private conversations so that there was a constant babble hanging over the room, but it stilled when Hawke returned to the piano and there was a smattering of applause as he sat down.

Hawke paused for just a moment, then began to play Tchaikovsky's Piano Concerto Number 1.

Chapter 23

LUCIANO APOLLONI WAS STANDING ON THE
riverbank in Cape Girardeau, Missouri. There were at least
one hundred others waiting on the levee for the *Delta Mist*.
They weren't passengers waiting to board the boat, they were
just residents of the town, here to celebrate the occasion. The
arrival of one of the passenger-carrying steamboats was always a big event in the life of the small river town.

When the boat came into view, the Cape Girardeau city
band began playing. The boat answered with several blasts
from its whistle, then it started putting in.

As Apolloni stood on the bank with the others, he checked
the telegram again.

*Rachel on Delta Mist Stop with Piano Player
Stop Do Both Stop Tangeleno*

Because the message was rather cryptic, it would not mean
that much to the telegraphers who transmitted it. But Apolloni knew exactly what the word "do" meant. He knew, also,
that if he killed both of them, he would be well rewarded.

Apolloni put the telegram in his pocket, then took the ticket he had bought for his own passage and walked down to the edge of the river.

"Sir, please step back until the boat has fully landed," one of the workers said.

"Yes, of course," Apolloni replied with a friendly smile. He did not want to do anything that would cause someone to remember him.

When the boat landed, its pilot added power and the stern wheel whirled rapidly, beating the brown Mississippi River water into a boiling froth. That had the effect of pegging the boat against the shore, holding it there while a big black deckhand stood at the bow and tossed over a rope that was as thick as a man's wrist. Workers on the shore took the rope, then wrapped it several times around a stanchion.

Not until secondary lines were thrown over and looped through a series of rings did the engines stop. Now the boat sat securely tied against the riverbank, a multitiered white edifice that looked like a floating hotel. Wisps of steam drifted away from the relief valves and a black ribbon of smoke curled up from the twin chimneys, indicating that the fireman was keeping the steam up. A sign was stretched between the two stacks. The name of the boat was written in red, outlined in gold and black.

DELTA MIST
PORT OF NEW ORLEANS
CAPTAIN E. P. ST. CYR

After that, the gangplank was lowered and a man, his wife, and two young boys came down the bouncing board. When they reached the bank, an elderly woman rushed forward to embrace them.

The boat purser came to the head of the gangplank and looked around for a moment before yelling down at the worker who had ordered Apolloni to step back.

"How many passengers are we picking up, Greg? And where bound?"

"Seven, for all points north," Greg called back.

"You got 'em all ticketed?"

"Aye."

"All right," the purser replied. "Start 'em up. We may as well get loaded."

Raising a megaphone to his lips, the boat official on the ground called out loudly.

"Passengers holding tickets for Ste. Genevieve, Perryville, St. Louis, and all points north may board now!"

Apolloni moved into line with the other six boarding passengers, climbed the gangplank, then handed his ticket to the purser.

"Welcome aboard, Mr. Apolloni," the purser said, reading the name on the ticket. "You'll be in Cabin E-4. Any questions?"

"I heard this boat has a piano player," Apolloni said. "Is that true?"

The purser looked up in surprise.

"Well, yes, it is true," he replied. "But how did you hear about him? We just put him on a week ago, down in New Orleans. This is his first trip upriver."

"I received a telegram from a friend who said that you had hired a good piano player. I thought it might make the trip to St. Louis more pleasant if we had some good music to listen to."

"Well, I don't think you will be disappointed. He is an outstanding piano player," the purser said. "But don't just take my word for it. You can judge for yourself when you have dinner tonight. He always plays in the salon for the evening meals."

"Good, good," Apolloni said. "I shall look forward to hearing him."

Apolloni went to his room, took out his knife, and began to sharpen it. The first thing he would have to do is identify the woman named Rachel. Once he had her located, he would wait until nightfall, find the opportunity to slit her throat, then drop her over into the river.

It was early evening, and the boat had just resumed its trip upriver after stopping at Perryville. Apolloni was in the back of the salon eating his dinner and listening to the piano music when the purser happened by his table.

"Ah, Mr. Apolloni, I hope you are enjoying the music," he said.

"Yes, I am," Apolloni replied.

"Would you like to meet him? He's not only a talented pianist, he is also very gracious to our passengers."

"No, thank you."

"He'll probably take a break after the next song. That would give you an excellent opportunity to meet him. I'll introduce you. You won't be imposing on him," the purser said.

"No!" Apolloni said more sharply. Then, when he saw the way the purser reacted to his reply, he softened it with a smile. "I mean, I'm very shy around new people. I'd rather just sit back here and listen. I hope you understand."

"Of course I understand," the purser said, mollified by Apolloni's smile and explanation. "My wife is the same way. You just sit here and enjoy your meal and the music. And if there is anything I can do for you, just let me know."

"Thank you," Apolloni said.

As the purser walked away, Apolloni went back to his dinner. He had to admit that the pianist was very good. He was so good that it would be a shame to have to kill him. But Tangeleno's telegram had been very specific. He was to "do" both of them, and business was business.

When this piece was finished, several of the diners went up to talk to the piano player. One of the diners was a very beautiful young woman, who fit the description of Rachel. Apolloni noticed that while the others returned to their tables or left the salon entirely, she hung around. There seemed to be a connection of some sort between them.

The purser happened to walk by the table again and Apolloni called out to him.

"Yes, sir, Mr. Apolloni, what can I do for you?"

"Do you know that woman's name?" Apolloni asked, pointing to the blonde who was standing by the piano.

The purser chuckled. "I can see why you might be interested. She is truly a lovely thing, isn't she?" the purser replied.

"Is she the piano player's, uh, companion?"

"They do seem to be getting along quite well, don't they? But I don't believe there is really any connection. I mean, she didn't even come onboard until Caruthersville. I believe her name is Smith. Miss Smith."

"What is her first name?"

"My—and you said you were the shy one," the purser said. "Well, I'm not supposed to do this, but her name is Rachel. Rachel Smith."

"Rachel?"

"Yes."

"Thank you."

"Good luck with her, Mr. Apolloni," the purser said as he walked away. He laughed again. "As they say, hope springs eternal."

Rachel, Apolloni thought. Yes, this was the one. He didn't

know what such a beautiful girl could possibly have done to cause Tangeleno to require that she be killed, but his wasn't to question why.

When Hawke heard a light knock, he knew who it would be even before he opened the door. He had not yet gone to bed because he was rearranging a piece of music for tomorrow evening. He set the music aside, then walked over to the door.

"Rachel?" he called quietly.

"Yes," Rachel replied.

Hawke opened the door, causing a wedge of light from the companionway to spill into his cabin. Rachel was standing in the doorway.

"So much for the mystery," she said. "How did you know it was me?"

"Because you are the one I wanted it to be," Hawke said.

"Aren't you the smooth talker, though?" she asked. "Are you going to ask me in?"

Hawke stepped aside. "Yes, of course I am. Come in," he said.

Rachel stepped into the room, then Hawke closed the door behind her.

"Would you like a glass of wine?" Hawke asked, pointing toward a bottle.

"Yes, that would be nice, thank you." Rachel walked over to sit on the edge of Hawke's bunk and she waited while he poured two glasses of wine. He brought the glasses over, then handed one to her.

"What shall we toast?" Rachel asked.

"How about a toast for Georgia and memories?" Hawke suggested.

To Hawke's surprise, Rachel shook her head. "There's nothing about Georgia I want to remember," she said.

"All right, then you make the toast."

"To Fancy," Rachel said, holding out her glass. The glass captured a beam of light from the lantern and the burgundy fired brilliantly.

"To Fancy," Hawke replied.

They drank their wine, then Rachel set her glass down.

"Mason, while you were at the Evening Star, why did you never come visit me?"

"It wasn't just you. I didn't visit any of the girls," Hawke replied.

"I know." Rachel smiled. "And that's the only reason I'm not angry with you. If you had visited one of the others, but not me, I wouldn't even be talking to you now."

"I was working there. I didn't think it was my place."

"Oh, for heaven's sake. It wouldn't have cost you anything."

"It's not that. It's just that I didn't deem it appropriate to mix business with . . . well, business," Hawke said with a little chuckle.

"We're not working together now," Rachel said. "At least not yet."

Even as she was talking, Rachel began slipping out of the dress she was wearing and Hawke saw that she had on nothing but a silk-muslin chemise underneath. The soft light of the lantern highlighted the thin garment, making it shimmer as if by its own golden light. The chemise draped her form like a filmy curtain, and the nipples of her breasts stood out in bold relief.

"Are you just going to stand there and stare at me? Are you going to join me or do you want me to put my clothes back on and leave?"

Hawke smiled. "Between the two choices you just offered, I would rather join you," Hawke said. He leaned down and kissed her.

For just a second Rachel hesitated. Whores never kissed. But she wasn't a whore now, so this was different. She opened her lips to his kiss.

"Mason," Rachel whimpered.

"Yes?"

"I . . . I have a confession to make."

"Wait. You're not going to tell me you aren't a virgin, are you?" Hawke asked.

Rachel looked at him with a shocked expression on her face, then, seeing the devilment in his eyes, she laughed out loud.

"You are awful!" she said.

"What is your confession?"

"I want to do this. I've never done this before because I wanted to."

Hawke took the lead then, kissing her a second time, more urgently than before. She responded by pushing her body against his.

Hawke sat on the bed beside her, then gently pushed her down. He kissed her again, once more pulling her body against his, feeling her softness against the hardness of his muscles. His kisses became more demanding and Rachel became more responsive, positioning herself here and moving herself there to accommodate him.

This was all new to Rachel. Although she had been with many men, more men than she could count, she had never done anything more than spread her legs and bear the ordeal. Now she was experiencing a sensation unlike anything she had ever felt before. It was as if hot tea was flowing through her veins. Is this what the other girls talked about when they said that there times when they actually enjoyed it? Why had she never felt anything like this before? She used the tip of her tongue to dart across his lips, then dip into his mouth.

* * *

The warmth Hawke felt erupted now to a raging inferno, and he began to pull at the hem of Rachel's chemise while removing his own clothes until they were naked against each other.

Hawke moved his hard demanding body over her soft yielding thighs and, poised above her, paused for a moment as if prolonging the experience. Then he went ahead.

Chapter 24

WHEN APOLLONI SAW RACHEL WALKING DOWN the passageway, he looked around quickly for a place to get out of sight. Just off the passageway was a small alcove that contained a wound-up fire hose and a red-handled axe. It was deep enough to allow Apolloni to hide, so he stepped into it.

When Rachel reached this end of the passageway, it would be a simple thing to step out and grab her, then pull her out onto the deck. One quick slice across her throat is all he would need—and it would be over.

But she didn't come all the way to this end. Instead, Apolloni heard a knock and, leaning out to look around the corner, he saw the door open to the piano player's room. The woman and the piano player spoke only for a second, then she went inside.

Apolloni waited for a few minutes longer, expecting her to come out again. When she didn't, he grew frustrated and sneaked back down the narrow companionway, stopping just outside the door. He listened carefully to see if he could hear anything.

He heard nothing.

What could possibly be going on in there? Then, realizing what it must be, he smiled. For a moment he considered going in right now, killing the piano player, and then having his way with the woman before he killed her. The thought of it gave him an erection and he rubbed himself through his pants as he contemplated the pleasure of it.

As he continued to think about it, though, he realized that his plan wouldn't work. He would have to kill the piano player first and while he was killing him, the woman was sure to call out, perhaps even scream.

Pleasure would have to wait. He was here to do a job, and he didn't intend to let anything get in his way. He moved down to the end of the passageway again, then stepped back into the fire hose alcove to wait for them to finish. He knew that she would have to pass by him to get to her own cabin.

"I hope you are enjoying this," he said under his breath. "Because this will be the last time for you."

He waited for almost an hour, then, thinking that she might spend the entire night in the room with him, was about to give up. He stepped out of the alcove just as he heard the door open and, quickly, he stepped back into the alcove again.

Looking carefully around the corner of the alcove, he saw the woman by the light of the wall-mounted lantern. He couldn't see the man because of the door, but when she leaned slightly forward, he knew they must be sharing their last kiss.

The door closed and the woman started toward her own cabin. Apolloni pulled his knife out and let his fingers wrap familiarly, almost caressingly, around the handle.

* * *

Hawke turned away from the door and was about to go to bed when he saw that Rachel had left her shawl. Grabbing it, he opened the door. He was going to call out to her, but thought it might disturb some of the other passengers, to say nothing of embarrassing Rachel. So, grabbing the shawl, he started down the passageway toward her.

That was when he saw a man suddenly step out into the little hallway. At first, he thought it was just a coincidence and that the man had come from a room. He hesitated, not only because he didn't want to embarrass Rachel, but because he was only half-dressed. Then he saw that the man was holding a knife in his right hand.

Hawke moved quickly and silently, coming up behind the assailant, grabbed the man's shoulder, and spun him around.

"What?" the assailant gasped, startled by Hawke's action. Then, seeing that his adversary was the piano player, he smiled.

"Oh!" Rachel gasped when she saw what was going on.

"Rachel, get out of here!" Hawke said.

Rachel moved out of the way, but she couldn't leave.

"Well now, piano player," he said. "I'd planned to kill both of you. You've just made it easy for me."

The assailant bent his knees slightly, leaned forward at the waist, and held his knife in his right hand, palm up, in front of him. He moved it in tiny circles, like the head of a coiled snake. With his left hand, he curled his fingers in invitation.

"Come on, piano player," he said in a low hissing tone. "Come get a taste of Apolloni's blade."

Hawke was unarmed and he had no choice but to start backing up as Apolloni advanced. Apolloni made one sweeping slice with his knife and Hawke skipped back out of the way. He didn't skip back far enough, though, and the tip of the blade opened up a cut on his side.

"Oh, Mason!" Rachel called out in concern.

Although the cut wasn't very deep, it looked bad because blood began flowing freely all along the length of the wound. Hawke's undershirt turned red.

"Oh, damn, that hurt, didn't it?" Apolloni taunted.

Hawke continued to back up while Apolloni pressed his advantage. Then, as he drew even with the fire hose alcove, Hawke reached in and grabbed the hose. Jerking it off the reel, he swung the nozzle toward Apolloni, hitting him in the chest. Caught unaware, Apolloni staggered back and Hawke leaped toward him, grabbing the knife hand.

As the two men struggled for the knife, Rachel watched the drama unfold before her.

Nobody said a word as the two men struggled in the dark. The only sounds were the sounds of heavy breathing, grunting, and the scraping of feet against the deck as they fought.

Rachel saw Apolloni make a thrust down low, then she saw him smile and she almost screamed. But before she could make a sound, the smile left the assailant's face to be replaced with a look of pain and surprise as Hawke stepped away from him.

Apolloni turned toward Rachel and she saw the knife sticking out of his stomach. He started toward her and Hawke quickly stepped in between them. Apolloni took two more staggering steps, then he collapsed against Hawke. Hawke grabbed Apolloni by his belt and collar, then lifted him up to the top of the deck railing. He held him there for just a second before he dropped him over.

Apolloni fell into the water with a *splash,* though the splash was almost lost in the churning beat of the stern wheel that turned behind them.

"Oh, Mason, you are hurt!"

"It's not too bad," Hawke assured her. "The cut isn't deep."

Rachel went into his arms and he held her, feeling her quivering with fright.

"Did you recognize him?" Hawke asked.

"No. I saw him when he got on the boat, but I had never seen him before."

"He had to be working for Tangeleno," Hawke said. "And you are right, this Mafia thing seems to go beyond New Orleans."

As the *Delta Mist* beat its way upriver, two giant mirrored lanterns, sitting on top of the pilot house, sent powerful beams stabbing out onto the darkness ahead of the boat. A third beam was being maneuvered by one of the crewmen and it moved from one side of the river to the other. Perhaps to investigate the splashing sound, the beam passed over to this side.

Hawke pulled Rachel back out of the way so that they wouldn't be picked up by the beam as it played upon the surface of the water. He saw it flit quickly across Apolloni's body, now floating facedown and drifting toward the riverbank, away from the boat. Fortunately, the light operator did not seem to notice it. Without hesitation, the beam continued to work across the surface of the water, picking out floating logs and other river obstructions.

Rachel shivered.

"Are you cold?"

"A little," she said. "Mason, what am I going to do? I can't hide from these people for the rest of my life."

"You won't have to."

"What do you mean, I won't have to? They were after me in Memphis, they came after me here on the boat. When is it going to stop?"

"It will stop when I kill every son of a bitch they send after you," Hawke promised.

Rachel chuckled quietly. "You know, if anyone else told

me that, I would pass it off as just talk. But I really believe you could do that."

"I not only can do it, I will do it," Hawke promised. "Come along. I'll see you to your cabin."

Chapter 25

TANGELENO AND VIZZINI STEPPED DOWN FROM the train on to the platform at the Bellefont depot. With their bowler hats and three-piece suits, they stood out among the farmers and cowboys—and even the townspeople.

To the casual observer, they looked like salesmen from the East, perhaps of spirits or ladies' notions. No one could possibly believe that, between them, they could account for more than twenty killings.

The two men waited until their suitcases were off-loaded from the train, then, picking them up, walked out to the edge of the platform to examine the town.

The first thing they noticed was the smell. The streets and roads of New Orleans were paved with brick and cobblestone, and they were swept clean every day so that the odor was kept down.

Here, the dirt streets were covered with layer upon layer of horse droppings, which, over time, broke down into an emulsified muck. The result was a stench that was so strong it overpowered everything.

"Holy shit," Vizzini said, putting his hand to his nose. "What the hell is that smell?"

"You called it," Tangeleno said with a little chuckle. "It's shit, all right, but I don't know how holy it is."

Fighting the odor as best they could by breathing in short breaths, the two men crossed the street to check in to the Railroad Hotel. "I would like a room with a view of the depot," Vizzini said.

The clerk chuckled. "That won't be hard," he said. "Most folks want to get away from the depot because of the sound. And will you be sharing a room?"

"Hell no. Put me in the back," Tangeleno said.

"Very good, sir." The clerk took a key down from a board of hooks and keys. "You're in Room 22," he said to Vizzini. "Go upstairs, then come all the way back to the front. And you will be in Room 28. It is at the very back," he said to Tangeleno.

In his room Tangeleno took off his jacket, poured water into the basin, and washed his face and hands. Although it did not look as if he was armed, removing his jacket revealed a rather unique shoulder holster that kept his pistol covered by his jacket.

After washing his face and hands, Tangeleno combed his hair, then put his jacket on. Walking down to the end of the hall, he started to knock on Vizzini's door to see if he wanted to go with him, but decided against it. He had spent the last several days with him on the train coming out. It would be good to be away from Vizzini for a while.

Downstairs, Tangeleno stepped up to the desk.

"Where is the closest place to get a drink?" he asked.

"That would be the Brown Dirt Saloon," the desk clerk replied. "Go out the front door, then across the street. It's three buildings down to the right. You can't miss it."

"Thanks."

When Tangeleno went out front, he saw that the hotel was right next door to Smalley's Mercantile.

Recognizing the name Smalley from the letters he and Vizzini had taken from the whore's room, he decided to take a look inside.

A sign in front of the store read:

GOODS FOR ALL MANKIND.
QUALITY HIGH. PRICES LOW.

He went into the door and a young woman came to the front, answering the tinkling of the small door-activated bell.

When Louise Smalley saw Joseph Tangeleno standing just inside the door of her store, she stopped and put her hand to her heart. She knew who he was, because she remembered him from her days at the House of the Evening Star.

But what was he doing here? Had he come to expose her?

Louise wasn't worried about him exposing her to her husband. Eddie already knew about her past. But if Tangeleno let the rest of the town know about her, it could cause problems.

Hesitantly, warily, she went up to him. She was very careful not to let him know that she had recognized him.

"May I help you?" she asked.

"No," he answered. "I'm just new to your town and I am looking around," Tangeleno said.

Louise smiled pleasantly. "Well, as you can see, we have quite a well-stocked store here. And if there is something you need that we don't have, we can always order it and, by train, have it in within two weeks."

"Nice store," Tangeleno said as he continued to look around.

It did not appear to Louise that Tangeleno recognized her. Was that possible?

She had never, personally, gone up to her room with Tangeleno, but she had seen him in the parlor several times. Maybe, since they had never actually been together, he didn't recognize her.

"I'm doing an inventory, but if there is anything I can help you with, let me know," Louise said, anxious to get away before he started studying her too closely.

"Thank you," Tangeleno replied. He walked around the store for a moment, paused to turn the crank on a meat grinder, shrugged, then left.

"Eddie?" Louise called.

"Yes, dear, what is it?" her husband answered, coming to the front of the store.

Louise was going to tell him about the Italian she recognized from New Orleans, but decided against it. Maybe she was concerned about nothing. After all, it didn't seem that he had recognized her.

"Oh, nothing, here it is," she said, picking up a pencil. "I just couldn't remember where I left this."

Eddie chuckled and kissed her. "You would lose your head if it wasn't attached," he teased as he returned to what he was doing.

Other than Eddie, the only people in town who knew about her background were the two "soiled doves" she had befriended. She would have to tell them about Tangeleno and make certain they didn't give her away.

Tangeleno did not remember the name Louise, but he did remember having seen this woman before. He chuckled to himself. Here she was, passing herself off as an innocent store clerk. He was sure she didn't want the town to know that she was once a whore. That might provide Vizzini and him with a little edge if he needed her help in anything.

Once more picking his way through the malodorous ooze, Tangeleno crossed the street. Stepping up onto the boardwalk in front of the Brown Dirt Saloon, he made use of a brush shoe scraper that was nailed to the boardwalk, just for that purpose. He stood for a moment outside the batwing doors, looking in to the shadowed interior of the saloon.

Four or five rough-looking and unkempt men were in the bar when Tangeleno went in, and they looked at him pointedly, taking note of the way he was dressed. He knew from the expressions on their faces that they regarded him as a dandy, someone of no consequence. He hoped one of them would challenge him. If he was going to get any respect in this town, he would have to establish himself right away. And the easiest way to do that would be to respond to a challenge.

Unlike the polished bars in the saloons and inns of New Orleans, this bar was made of unpainted rip-sawed lumber. Its only concession to decorum was to place towels in rings spaced about five feet apart on the customer side of the bar. But the towels looked as if they had not been changed in months, if ever, so their very filth negated the effect of having them there.

When Tangeleno stepped up to the bar, the bartender, with a dirty towel thrown across one shoulder, moved down to him.

"Yeah?" he said.

"Chianti," Tangeleno ordered.

The bartender was chewing on a snuff-dipping stick. "What'd you say?" he asked around the edge of the stick.

"I said I would like a glass of Chianti, please," Tangeleno said.

"Chianti?" The bartender pulled the stick from his mouth and a little string of brown spittle stretched between the stick and his lips before it broke. "Mister, I don't have any idea in hell what a Chianti is," he said.

"It is a wine," Tangeleno explained. "An Italian wine."

"Yeah, well, we ain't got no wine here. All we got here is beer and whiskey. You want beer or whiskey, I can accommodate you."

"I'll have a beer," he said.

There was a man standing at the other end of the bar, and he had watched the exchange between Tangeleno and the bartender with a look of amusement on his face.

"Hey, dandy man," he called down to him. "Do you think you're too good for beer or whiskey?"

Tangeleno looked at the man who had just challenged him.

"Are you talking to me?" he asked.

"Am I talking to you? Hell yeah, I'm talking to you. Do you see any other dandy men in here?"

"I prefer wine, but beer will do," Tangeleno said.

"I don't know any man who drinks wine," the belligerent one said. "I know lots of women, but I don't know any men who drink wine."

"What is your name?" Tangeleno asked.

"What?"

"What is your name?"

"The name is Deekus. Not that it'll make any difference to you. It ain't like me'n you's goin' to be friends. I don't make friends with dandy men."

The others in the saloon laughed at Tangeleno's expense.

"Deekus. Is that a first name or a last name?"

"It's the only name you need to know," Deekus said.

Tangeleno turned then so that he was directly facing Deekus. "Well, Deekus, my name is Tangeleno," he said. "You can call me Mr. Tangeleno."

"Ha! Like I'm gong to call you 'mister,'" Deekus said with a raucous laugh.

"Deekus, I had hoped I was going to be able to make you listen to reason, but it is clear that I won't."

Tangeleno smiled, a cold, brittle smile, as he enjoyed the fact that Deekus had no idea what the words "listen to reason" meant to those who understand their significance.

Deekus, who had been laughing ever since this encounter started, now laughed so hard that he slapped his hand on the bar. "You want me to listen to reason, do you, dandy man?" He pointed at Tangeleno's hat.

"Where did you find that thing?" he asked. "Under some whore's bed? You know what I think, mister? I think that looks a lot more like a whore's piss pot than a hat."

Tangeleno took off his bowler and looked inside it for a moment.

"*Lei ha ragione, sembra la pentola di piscia che io ho preso da sotto il letto della Sua prostituta di una madre.*"

"What? What did you say? I don't understand Mex talk."

"It wasn't Spanish, it was Italian," Tangeleno said. "And I will interpret. What I said was: 'You are right. It does look like the piss pot that I took from under the bed of your whore of a mother.'"

Deekus quit laughing and the expression on his face turned to rage.

"What? Why, you dandified son of a bitch! I'm going to blow you to hell!" Deekus said, drawing his pistol. He had the pistol about half-drawn when Tangeleno suddenly reached down into his hat and pulled out a knife. With barely more than a flip of his wrist, he threw the knife. It turned over once in midair, then buried itself in Deekus's chest.

The expression of rage turned to one of shock as Deekus dropped his pistol and looked down at the knife that was protruding from his chest. Deekus collapsed.

"Deekus!" one of the other men in the saloon yelled. Hurrying over to him, he knelt beside the fallen cowboy. "Deekus!" he said again.

Deekus lay on the floor, his eyes open but sightless. The man beside Deekus stood up then and glared at Tangeleno.

"Mister, you just killed my brother," he said.

"Did I? Well, he needed killing." Putting his hand in under his jacket, Deekus wrapped his fingers around the butt of the small but deadly Belgian 7 mm Pinfire revolver that nestled in his shoulder holster.

"You ain't goin' to find me that easy to kill," the brother said.

"Farley, you watched this go down same as did ever'one else," the bartender said. "Deekus egged on this here foreign feller. Besides, Deekus drew on him 'cause he didn't think he was armed. Now, why don't you go down and get the undertaker so's you can give your brother a decent burial."

"I'll go get the undertaker," Farley said. "Soon as I take care of the Mexican here."

"I'm not Mexican," Tangeleno said.

"You are about to be a dead Mexican," Farley said.

"Farley, if you kill him, you'll be hung for murder, sure as a gun is iron. He's done throwed his knife. He ain't even armed now."

"I can fix that," Farley said. Bending down again, he picked up his brother's pistol, then he put it on the bar and gave it a push. It made a scraping noise as it slid down the bar, where it stopped and rocked back and forth in front of Tangeleno. Tangeleno stared pointedly. "There you go, mister. Pick it up anytime you're ready."

"I don't care to use that gun," Tangeleno said.

"Yeah, well, you don't have no choice," Farley said. "It's the only gun you've got."

Farley stepped away from the bar, then let his right hand hang down, flexing his fingers open and closed just over the handle of his pistol.

"Farley, you don't want to do this," the bartender said.

"Stay out of this, Ely. This here ain't none of your concern. This is between me and this here Mexican."

"I'm not Mexican," Tangeleno said again.

"Ain't goin' to do you no good to keep your hand under your coat like that," Farley said. "I'm going to start countin'. And when I reach three, I'm going to shoot you whether you've reached for that gun or not. One."

The confrontation between Tangeleno and Deekus had all happened so quickly that nobody in the saloon had time to react. But this was playing out with all the timing and choreography of a staged melodrama.

"Two."

Tangeleno had still not taken his hand out from under his jacket.

"Three!" Farley shouted, going for his gun.

Suddenly, and to the total surprise of everyone in the room, Tangeleno took his hand out from under his jacket and there was a gun in his hand.

Farley halted in middraw. He had been keeping his eyes on the gun on the bar, and he was totally shocked to see a pistol in Tangeleno's hand.

Tangeleno smiled, a cold, evil smile. He pulled the trigger and the gun boomed, the sound of the gunshot very loud in the closed confines of the room.

A hole appeared in Farley's chest, and he looked down at it, then back at Tangeleno, his face registering the same surprise as had his brother's a few minutes earlier. Smoke curled up from the barrel of Tangeleno's gun, then formed an acrid-blue cloud to hover over the room.

"You son of . . ." Farley said. He tried to raise his pistol but before he could do so, his eyes rolled back in his head and he fell back onto the body of his brother.

So taken aback was everyone by what they had just seen that, for a long moment, no one said a word. It was Tangeleno who broke the silence.

"I told you, I didn't want to use that gun," Tangeleno said.

Tangeleno put his pistol back in the shoulder holster, then turned to the bartender.

"I'll have that beer now," he said.

"Yes, sir!" the bartender replied, as awestruck as everyone else by what he had just seen.

When the little bell in Smalley's Mercantile called Louise to the front again, she saw Maggie coming into the store. Maggie, who was one of the whores who worked out of the Brown Dirt Saloon, knew about Louise's background and the two women had become friends.

"Hello, Maggie," Louise said, greeting her warmly.

"Louise," Maggie said, eager to share her news. "Did you hear what happened in the saloon while ago?"

"No."

"Deekus and Farley Carter got themselves killed."

"Both of them got killed?"

"Yes."

"That's a shame," Louise said. "But, from what people say about Deekus, it doesn't come as that big of a surprise. He was always trying to provoke someone into doing something. You say both of them were killed? Good heavens, they didn't kill each other, did they?"

"No," Maggie said. "Like you said, Deekus was always provoking someone. Only today, I guess he provoked the wrong one."

"Was it murder?"

"No, the sheriff has already come over and talked to

everyone, and they all agree on what happened. Deekus got himself killed, then Farley stepped in, and the little Italian fella killed him too."

Louise gasped. "You say it was an Italian man who did it?"

"Yes. That's what surprised everyone. I mean, who would've thought a little fella like that could handle both Deekus and Farley?"

"Oh, Maggie," Louise said, the expression on her face one of fear. "Please don't tell anyone that I told you, but I know that man. His name is Tangeleno."

"Tangeleno, yes, that's what he said. How do you know him?"

"I knew him in New Orleans. He is more dangerous than a rattlesnake. Don't cross him—ever."

"Don't worry, I won't."

Chapter 26

LATE IN THE AFTERNOON OF THE THIRD DAY AFTER the incident with Apolloni, the Delta Mist put in at Leclede's Landing in St. Louis. Unlike all their stops at the small towns downriver where they were the only boat tied up, here in St. Louis it was difficult to find a berthing place. That was because there were at least ten other passenger-carrying boats and an even greater number of barges and cargo boats crowded against the bank. In addition, several boats were parked just offshore, the strong, six mile per hour current causing them to pull hard against their anchors.

Fully half the boats were Missouri River boats, easily identified because they had much shallower drafts and smaller superstructures. The riverbank was crowded, not by the curious, but by those people whose commerce required their presence. It was also a noisy place, with whistles, bells, chugging steam engines, the slap of paddles against the water and the clatter of horse, mule, and oxen hooves, as well as iron-rimmed wheels rolling over cobblestone as the large wagons took on or offloaded the cargoes carried by the boats.

Hawke was in his cabin, preparing to disembark. Although

there was a small red line on his side, the result of his encounter with Apolloni, the cut was so light that it had already
closed and required no attention.

"Mason, are you ready?"

Hawke had left the door to his cabin open and, looking
around, he saw Rachel standing there. Her suitcase was beside her.

"Yes," Hawke said, putting on his hat. Going to the door, he
picked up her suitcase so that he was carrying both of them.

There were several passengers getting off in St. Louis,
and Hawke and Rachel stood patiently in line as they waited
for the crowd to dissipate. That was when the purser came up
to them.

"I'm asking everyone onboard the same question," he said.
"Have either of you seen Mr. Apolloni?"

"Apolloni?" Hawke replied. He shook his head. "I don't
think I know him."

"Well, there's no reason you should," the purser said. "But
he did seem interested in your music—and quite intrigued
with you, Miss Smith."

"With me?"

"Yes, he found you very attractive. Of course, that's not
all that surprising. I can't imagine anyone not finding you
attractive."

"Why, thank you," Rachel said.

"Where is Mr. Apolloni now?" Hawke asked. "I would be
glad to meet him."

"Well, that's just it," the purser said. "I don't know where
he is. I haven't seen him in a couple of days and he is supposed to disembark here. When I sent a steward to check his
cabin, the steward reports that it was not slept in last night."

"Maybe he got off before we reached St. Louis," Hawke
suggested.

"Yes, there is that possibility, of course," the purser said.

"There is also the possibility that he may have fallen over-board during the night."

"Oh, let's hope not," Hawke said.

"Indeed," the purser agreed. He reached out to shake Hawke's hand. "I must say, Mr. Hawke, it has been a pleasure having you aboard. I shall miss all the beautiful music."

"Thank you very much. Playing for your passengers has been quite a pleasant experience," Hawke said.

As the purser moved on to ask others about Apolloni, the line ahead of them cleared, and the two of them walked down the gangplank and to set foot on the riverbank in St. Louis, Missouri.

Two men were standing in the crowd, watching the passengers as they left the boat. They were close enough to the gangplank to hear the purser exchange a few words with everyone who debarked. Their interest perked when they heard the reference to the music.

"That's him, Ned," one of the men said. He pointed to Hawke. "That's the piano player."

"Luby, get your hand down," Ned said, slapping the hand away. "You want him to see you pointing at him?"

"No, I reckon not," Luby said sheepishly. "So what do we do now?"

"We follow them," Ned said.

In addition to Ned and Luby, there was yet another person in the crowd who had watched, with interest, as the passengers disembarked. Dominico Dallipiccola was too far away from the boat to hear the purser or to hear the conversation between Ned and Luby. But when he saw their interest in a man and woman who seemed to be traveling together, he smiled and twirled his mustache. That had to be the two people Tangeleno was interested in.

If this works, he would become Don Dallipiccola, head of the St. Louis Family. Don Dallipiccola, my respects to you, Godfather, he thought. Then he said the words aloud. *"Don Dallipiccola I miei rispetti a Lei, Padrinoa."*

Six months ago, with the blessings of Joseph Tangeleno, Dallipiccola had come upriver from New Orleans. His purpose in coming to St. Louis was to find Sicilian and Italian immigrants who would be interested in forming a Family. The problem was that, while there were many Italians and Sicilians in St. Louis, they were more interested in hard work and honest enterprise than they were in any organized criminal activity.

Frustrated by his inability to rally his own countrymen to his cause, Dallipiccola had to enlist outsiders. Ned and Luby were two of his more recent recruits.

But if they took care of this little assignment he had given them, he was certain that Tangeleno would be very generous, not only with money, but in recognizing the existence of the St. Louis Family with Dominico Dallipiccola as its head.

There were several hacks drawn up along North Wharf Street, and as Hawke and Rachel approached them, Hawke called out to one of the drivers. Responding to Hawke's hail, the driver snapped the reins over his horse and pulled out of line, driving up to stop in front of Hawke and Rachel.

"Take us to the railroad station," Hawke said as he put the two bags in the hack, then helped Rachel climb in.

"Yes, sir, that would be Union Station," the driver replied as he pulled out of the line.

It had recently rained in St. Louis and the horse's hooves made a staccato beat on the glistening wet pavement as the driver turned west on to Market Street, then maneuvered the hack through the traffic before bringing it to a stop under the Union Station porte cochere.

Paying the fare, Hawke and Rachel stepped down from the hack. They took no notice of the private carriage that stopped about twenty-five yards behind them.

"They will be buying tickets to Bellefont, Kansas," Dallapiccola said. "Find out which train."

"It don't make no difference which train," Ned said. "They won't never get on it."

"Nevertheless, find out which train," Dallapiccola said.

As Hawke and Rachel went inside the depot, they passed through a golden entry arch, under the mosaic-glass window, then climbed the great staircase to the Grand Hall from whose sixty-five-foot-high vaulted ceiling hung an enormous chandelier.

The floor of the Grand Hall teemed with humanity: men and women moving to or from trains, children laughing or crying. As the trains entered or departed from the great domed train shed, Hawke could feel the floor rumbling under his feet.

"Get us tickets to Bellefont on the Palace Car," Rachel said as she handed him some money. "Oh, and if you don't mind sharing a roomette with me, it will save money."

Hawke smiled. "In the interest of saving money, I will make the sacrifice."

Hawke stood in line until it was his turn at the ticket window.

"The train will depart from Track Number 8 at nine-thirty this evening," the ticket agent said as he slid the long multi-sectioned tickets across the counter.

As he walked away from the counter, he looked toward the huge clock that hung on the wall just beside the sign that read: TO TRAINS. It was nearly seven.

"What do you say we put our suitcases in a locker, then have our dinner?" Hawke suggested after he told Rachel what time the train would be leaving.

"Why, Mr. Hawke, are you engaging me for dinner?" Rachel asked coquettishly.

"I am."

"I accept."

They ate at a French restaurant on Olive, just a few blocks north of Union Station.

"How is the ham?" Rachel asked.

"It is quite good, madam."

"Then I think I will have *jambon et champignons*," Rachel said when the waiter approached their table.

"Excellent choice, madam," the waiter said. "The mushrooms are also particularly good. And you, sir?"

"Is your salmon fresh?" Hawke asked after examining the menu.

"*Oui, monsieur.* It comes by train, daily, packed in ice," the waiter replied.

"Very good. I'll have *les rillettes de saumon.*"

Rachel laughed as the waiter withdrew.

"What is so funny?"

"I had the thought that I would be able to impress you with my New Orleans French," she said. "But I should have known better. As I recall now, you went to France, didn't you? Just before the war?"

"Yes. I must confess, though, that my French is only barely passable."

Ned and Luby were in the same restaurant, sitting on the opposite side of the room keeping a close eye on Hawke and Rachel.

"I tell you what, Ned, I hope we aren't wasting our time with these two," one of them said. "What if they ain't the right ones?" Luby said.

"You heard what Dallapiccola said, didn't you? One was a whore, and the other was a piano player."

"Yeah, I heard him say that."

"You was there when the boat landed, same as me," Ned said. "And you heard the purser call this fella a piano player, right?"

"Yeah," Luby agreed.

"So we know he's a piano player. And if what we are lookin' for is a piano player and a whore travelin' together, then the woman sittin' there with him has to be the whore."

"What's the name of that fella down in New Orleans that wants 'em dead? Tangeleno or somethin' like that?" Luby asked.

"Hell, I don't know. Who can pronounce them names anyway?"

"How come, you reckon, the Italians want 'em dead?"

"I don't know, and I don't care, as long as Dallipiccola pays us the thousand dollars apiece he promised," Ned said.

"Hey, Ned, you think he'll really pay us?" Luby asked.

"Yeah, I've done things for him before. He'll pay. For some reason, them Italians is big on honor," Ned answered.

Across the room, Hawke and Rachel got up from their table.

"They're leaving," Luby said.

"Let's go," Ned replied.

Chapter 27

IT WAS QUITE DARK WHEN HAWKE AND RACHEL left the restaurant and a heavy fog had moved in off the river, making it very difficult to see more than just a few feet.

"Are you sure we are going the right way to get back to the depot?" Rachel asked.

"We can't get lost," Hawke said. "We came out on Twelfth Street. All we have to do is follow it right back to the depot."

"If you say so," Rachel said.

As they walked through the dark, foggy night, pedestrians would pop out of the fog in front of them, appearing and disappearing almost as if summoned and dispatched by some great wizard. Carriages drove by on the street, their presence acknowledged only by hoof falls and rolling wheels and the feathery glow of disembodied lanterns that seemed—somehow—to float by.

Rachel put both hands on Hawke's arm and held it tight.

"I don't mind admitting that I find this entire evening rather spooky," she said. "If I weren't with you, I would be frightened to death."

Almost as if in answer to her fear, two men suddenly

jumped out from an alley in front of them. Both men were brandishing knives and they stood in front of Hawke and Rachel.

"Well now, Luby, lookie here what we've got. Could it be the whore and the piano player?"

Luby chuckled. "That's what it looks like to me. But tell me, which one is the whore and which one is the piano player?"

Both men laughed at Luby's joke.

"Did Tangeleno send you?" Rachel asked in a frightened voice.

"Tangeleno? Hey, Ned, that's the name you said. You was right."

"Yeah," Ned said. "So, it looks like you can quit worryin' whether or not we got the right ones. I figure this just proves it."

"Oh, Mason," Rachel said, very frightened now. "Is this nightmare ever going to end?"

"How many more of you are there?" Hawke asked.

"How many more? No more. Just Luby and me. What makes you think we need anyone else?"

Hawke shook his head. "I'm not talking about how many of you are here," he said. "I mean, after I get rid of you two, who else will Tangeleno send after us?"

"What do you mean, after you get rid of us? Are you crazy?" Luby asked. He held his knife up. "We're the ones with the knives."

"Yes, but I'm the one with a gun," Hawke replied with a sardonic smile.

"You may have a gun, mister, but it ain't in your hand and . . ." Ned started, but gasped when he saw what happened next.

"Oh, but it *is* in my hand," Hawke said and, even as he spoke, the pistol was in his hand, the draw so fast that both assailants were caught completely off-guard.

"What the hell? How did you do that?" Luby asked.

"It doesn't matter how I did it. I did it," Hawke said. "Now take off your clothes."

"What?" Ned asked.

"I said take off your clothes, both of you."

"Mister, are you crazy? I ain't takin' off my clothes," Luby said.

"Don't worry about whether or not I'm crazy. What you should worry about is whether or not I will shoot you if you don't do what I say," Hawke said. He pulled the hammer back on his pistol. "And believe me, I will shoot you."

"I believe you," Luby said nervously. "Ned, I believe him."

"I'm glad you believe me," Hawke said. "Now take off your clothes."

"You can't ask us to do that. There's a woman here," Luby complained.

"You should have thought of that."

Suddenly Ned made a sudden lunge toward Hawke and Hawke fired. The bullet hit Ned's hand and he dropped his knife. It clattered as it fell to the cobblestone-paved street.

Luby dropped his knife as well and put up his hands.

"Neither one of us is armed now," Luby said anxiously.

"Take off your clothes," Hawke said again. "I figure if you two are wandering around St. Louis naked, you aren't as likely to get into trouble again."

The two men continued to glare at Hawke, but neither of them made an effort to comply with his demand.

Hawke pulled the trigger, and, with a yelp of pain, Luby put his hand up to his left ear. When he pulled it back, he was holding a little piece of flesh.

"You . . . you son of a bitch! You shot off my ear!"

"No, I didn't," Hawke said easily. "I just shot off a piece of your ear. But if you don't take off your clothes right now, I'm going to start carving pieces off both of you." He cocked the pistol and raised it up to point directly at Ned.

"No!" Ned said, holding out his hand as if, by that action, he could stop him. "No, don't shoot us no more!"

"Take off your clothes," Hawke ordered again.

Quickly, Ned and Luby slipped out of their clothes, then began piling them on the ground in front of them.

"No, not there," Hawke said. Using a wave of his pistol, he indicated a storm sewer on the curb. "Drop them down there."

"What the hell, mister? If we drop them down that hole, we never will get our clothes back," Luby said.

"That's right," Hawke said. "Maybe you should have thought of that before you came after us with knives. Do it."

Grumbling, Ned and Luby carried their discarded clothes over to the storm sewer and dropped them. Then they stood there in their long-handled underwear, glaring back at him.

"Take that off too," Hawke said.

"What?" Ned shouted angrily. "No, wait a minute. If we do that, that'll make us naked in front of the woman."

"I'm a whore, remember?" Rachel asked, laughing now at their plight. "You don't have anything that I haven't seen before."

A minute later both Ned and Luby were totally naked. They stood in front of Hawke and Rachel, holding their hands over their private parts.

"Now, you go that way," Hawke said, pointing off into the fog. "And we'll go this way. If I ever see you again, I will kill you on the spot."

Rachel laughed out loud as the two men ran off into the fog.

"I know I have no right to be laughing, I know Tangeleno is trying to kill me, but that was just too funny," she said.

"I'll give Tangeleno this," Hawke said. "He is persistent."

"How is he able to know where I am?" Rachel asked. "It's almost as if he knows where I'm going."

Because of the darkness and the fog, Ned and Luby were able to avoid being seen, simply by staying close to the buildings, moving through alleys, and stepping into doorways when necessary.

"This way," Ned said, pointing up one of the alleys.

"What do we want to go that way for? We live that way," Luby replied, pointing in the opposite direction.

"The Gandy Dancer is this way," Ned said.

"The Gandy Dancer?"

"That's a saloon where railroad workers hang out."

"I know what it is," Luby replied. "But I don't know why you want to go there. Are you plannin' on us just walkin' in there, butt-ass naked and orderin' a drink? Which, in case you ain't noticed, in addition to being naked, we also don't have no money."

"Have you ever been to the Gandy Dancer?"

"Yes, sure I have."

"Have you ever stepped out behind it to take a piss or something?"

"Yes."

"What did you see back there?" Ned asked.

"What do you mean, what did I see back there? I seen the privy."

"What else?"

"I didn't see nothin' else except . . . ," Luby replied, then he stopped in midsentence. "Drunks," he said. "I seen drunks."

"Drunks who are wearing clothes," Ned added.

Luby laughed. "Yeah, that's pretty smart, Ned. We can roll a drunk for his clothes, then we won't have to be goin' home butt-naked."

"We won't be goin' home. We're goin' to finish the job we started out to do."

"The hell with that," Luby said. "Let them damn Italians do their own killin'."

"You're that willing to turn your back on a thousand dollars, are you?" Ned asked. "Because if you are, I'll kill both of them myself and keep your share of the money."

"No," Luby said. "I was just talkin' is all. I'll come with you."

"I thought you might."

"We goin' to have to get us a couple of knives too," Luby said.

"To hell with that. We're goin' to use guns this time."

"Where we goin' to get guns?"

"Sikes Hardware store sells guns."

"Sikes ain't open now. They done closed for the day."

"Yeah, well, after a store is closed is the best time to shop if you don't have any money," Ned said.

"Yeah," Luby said. He laughed. "Yeah, you're right."

Chapter 28

DOMENICO DALLIPICCOLA WAS WAITING AT THE depot for Ned and Luby to come back and tell him that they had accomplished their mission. When they didn't come back to claim the money he had promised them, he knew that they had failed. Then, to his surprise, he saw Hawke and Rachel, obviously unharmed, get on the train.

Angry and frustrated, Dallipiccola bought a ticket on the same train. The old adage was right. If you wanted a thing done, it was best to do it yourself.

When he attempted to board the train, though, he was turned back at the gate.

"It's not time to board yet," he was told.

"I've seen others board this train."

"They're first-class passengers," the gate attendant said. "They are allowed to board early. Don't worry, you'll be called in plenty of time."

Grumbling, Dallipicolla returned to the waiting room to wait until it was time for him to board.

Inside the Palace Car the lanterns were all at their brightest as Hawke, Rachel, and the other first-class passengers prepared for the overnight trip across Missouri. Hawke and Rachel entered the car, passing a young mother, who was holding her baby in one hand while trying to put a hatbox in an overhead rack. She stretched as much as she could, but it was beyond her reach.

"Allow me," Hawke said. He smiled graciously at the lady and reached up to put the hatbox in place.

"Why, thank you, sir." Then, looking at Rachel, the young mother said, "Your husband is most kind."

"Yes, isn't he?" Rachel replied with a smile of her own.

Rachel and Hawke took a seat halfway back on the left side of the car. Hawke had bought a newspaper in the depot and, comfortably settled now, he began to look through it.

As Hawke read the paper, he happened to glance outside, where he saw two men walking between this track and the next track over. They were wearing the same kind of coveralls as the railroad workers, and he started to return to his newspaper when one of them just happened to turn his face so that Hawke could see it clearly.

It was Ned!

He looked again, just to make certain, and saw that it was indeed Ned and the other one was Luby. The same two men who had accosted them after dinner this evening were now walking alongside this very train. Somehow, they had managed to find clothes again, and not just any clothes, but the clothes of track workers, allowing them free access in the train shed.

Damn, Hawke thought. I should have killed both of them when I had the chance.

Hawke stood up. "You stay here," he said to Rachel.

"Where are you going?" Rachel asked, her voice showing her concern.

"I saw something outside that I need to check on," Hawke answered. He didn't give her any more information than that because he didn't want to alarm her. He smiled reassuringly. "I'll be right back," he promised. "Here, read the paper."

Rachel nodded, then began reading the paper as Hawke left the car.

Once he was outside, Hawke started walking alongside the train, carefully looking all around. He walked all the way up to the front of the train until he reached the engine, but the search proved fruitless. He didn't see the two men.

The engineer, the fireman, and the conductor were standing just outside the engine. The engineer had small chin whiskers that stuck, like a red flag, straight forward from the bottom of his chin. He was examining one of the driver-wheel bearings and the other two were looking over his shoulder.

The fireman had little circular scars on his face and neck. Hawke knew they weren't pox marks but were the result of tiny red-hot embers that, over the many years and miles of railroading, had blown back into his face and neck.

The conductor was the oldest of the three, clean shaven and with a head of snow-white hair. It was the conductor who noticed Hawke first.

"Here, mister, what are you doing out here?" the conductor asked authoritatively. "You aren't supposed to be here."

"My name's Hawke, and I'm a U.S. Marshal," Hawke lied, taking a chance that the conductor wouldn't ask for identification. "And I'm looking for two men that I believe I saw coming this way. They were wearing clothes like railroad workers, but I have reason to believe that they aren't workers."

"Two men? Yes, I saw them," the fireman said. "And now that you mention it, I didn't think I had ever seen them before." He pointed ahead. "They crossed the track just in front of the engine."

"Thanks," Hawke said. He crossed the track as well, then started back down the other side of the train, his eyes continuing to sweep back and forth.

He hadn't gone too far when he saw two men squatting down between the mail car and the first passenger car. He realized that they could be legitimate workers making some last-minute repair or modification to the train. But it could also be Ned and Luby, so he wanted to get a closer look at them to make sure.

"Excuse me, could I ask you two men a couple of questions?" he called.

Hawke's unexpected challenge caused the two men to jump. They disappeared between the two cars and Hawke started after them. He had gone no more than half a dozen steps, however, when one of them leaned back around the end of the car and raised his pistol.

It was Ned!

Ned fired at him and Hawke heard the bullet fly past his ear.

Drawing his own pistol, Hawke dropped to one knee and fired back. But because he didn't want to take a chance on damaging anything on the train or hurting any innocent bystander, he purposely shot low. His bullet struck sparks as it hit the rear truck of the car that was shielding the two men. The bullet then ricocheted under, and between the train cars, coming close enough to Ned and Luby to cause them to dash off to the other side.

The conductor, engineer, and fireman Hawke had just been talking to suddenly appeared alongside the engine, looking back along the train in curious wonder.

"What is it?" the engineer called. "What's going on? What's all the shooting?"

"Get down!" Hawke shouted, waving at them with his left hand. His right hand still held the pistol he had just fired. "All of you, down on the ground, now!"

Hawke didn't need to issue a second warning because the three men dived to the ground.

Hawke hurried to the gap between the mail car and the first

passenger car, then hopped over the coupling and crossed back to the side he had started on in the first place. Looking up and down the train, he saw that the two men were now four tracks over. He caught a glimpse of them, just as they were disappearing behind a freight train that was rolling out of the station.

Hawke ran across the tracks after them, but before he could reach them, another train moved between him and the intruders. The engineer of the train was leaning out the window of his cab, searching the track in front of him. The noise of his own train drowned out the sound of gunfire, and he had no idea who the men were, who were running up and down the tracks, or what they were doing. He gave them—and Hawke—only a passing glance, for, by now, he was rolling at a pretty good clip and the track ahead demanded all his attention.

Hawke heard still another train coming and he looked around to see a switch engine bearing down on him, going in the opposite direction as the train he was waiting to pass. If he hopped on it, he knew it would carry him to the end of the closing train, thus allowing the space between him and the two men he was chasing to open up faster. Waiting until the engine was by, he jumped on the ladder of one of the cars being shuffled about and rode it until the other train was clear. When he hopped back down, he had a good long look on the other side of the line of cars, but it was too late.

Ned and Luby were gone.

Frustrated that they had gotten away, Hawke returned to Track Number 8 where the *Kansas City Flyer* stood. He saw the engineer, the fireman, and another man examining the space between the cars where he had seen Ned and Luby.

"Did you get them, Mr. Hawke?" the engineer asked as Hawke returned.

"No," Hawke admitted. "I'm afraid they gave me the slip."

"Too bad," the engineer said.

"Charley, look here," the fireman said. The fireman was squatted down under the coupling.

"What you got, Wayne?" the engineer asked, squatting down beside him.

The fireman pointed to the rubber hose that was a part of the coupling. "It looks like they were trying to sabotage the train. They were cutting into the air-brake hose."

"Damn. Look at that, Mr. Bates," Charley said, pointing it out to the conductor.

The conductor also squatted down to examine the air-brake hose.

"And as you can see, they were being real smart about it too," Charley said. "They didn't cut far enough into the hose for it to rupture. But after twenty or thirty miles, what with the swaying and the strain between the cars and all, that line would have opened up and we would have lost all our air pressure. And, like as not, when that happened, it could've caused a wreck."

"Charley, how long will it take us to get the hose replaced?" Bates asked.

"Well, if they cut one of them, then they might have cut others. It'll take half an hour to an hour to fix this one and another half hour to check all the other hoses," the engineer replied. "That'll make us an hour and a half late getting started."

The conductor shook his head. "No, it'll make us three hours late," he said. "An hour from now, 969 will have the high iron coming into St. Louis. If we don't get started in the next fifteen minutes, we'll have to wait right here in the station for it."

"Then I reckon we're going to have to wait," the engineer said. "Because I ain't moving this train one inch until I'm satisfied that it's safe."

"I don't blame you, Charley," the conductor said. "And I'm not suggesting that you do."

The three train crewmen looked over at Hawke.

"What's this all about, Mr. Hawke?" the conductor asked.

"What do you mean?"

"I mean, what's goin' on between you and these fellas? And why would they try an' cut the brake hose on our train? Why would someone, of a pure purpose, do something that could get nearly everyone on this train killed?"

"There's nothing going on between me and them," Hawke lied. "I just happened to see a couple of men who were acting suspicious, so I thought I would check them out. That's all."

"Well, I'm glad you came along when you did," the engineer said.

"I'm just sorry they got away," Hawke said. "I'd better get back to the car now. My friend will be wondering what happened to me."

"You're a passenger on this train, are you?" Charley asked.

"Yes."

Charley nodded. "Well, seein' as someone is after this train, I'm glad you happened to be aboard."

"So am I," Bates agreed. "Mr. Hawke, if you see anything else . . . suspicious . . . please don't hesitate to let me know."

"You can count on it," Hawke said. He was grateful that he now had allies, even though they didn't know exactly what they were letting themselves in for.

When Hawke got back to the car, he expected to face a lot of questions, but was surprised to see that nobody seemed to have noticed his absence. Then he realized that with all the excitement of preparing for the departure, no one had been looking outside. Also the noise of the trains, echoing loudly under the covered train shed, had apparently drowned out any sound of gunshots.

"Is everything all right?" Rachel asked when Hawke took his seat beside her. Hawke knew then that not even she had suspected anything untoward had happened.

"Yes, everything is fine," Hawke answered.

"Oh, I found another story in here that you might be interested in," she said, handing him the newspaper, folded in such a way as to highlight the story.

BODY FOUND IN RIVER

Story filed by Eugene Field
special correspondent to the St. Louis
Journal

Hawke read the story, then handed the paper back to Rachel.

"That is the same man who tried to attack me, isn't it?" she asked.

"I would say so."

"Then why didn't the story say anything about the knife?"

"It probably fell out while he was in the river. And unless they examine the body very closely, the wound is so small that it wouldn't be that noticeable."

"It gives me the willies to think about it," Rachel said.

"Better him than you," Hawke replied.

The conductor came walking through the car then.

"Folks, we've had some delay. It's going to be another two hours before we pull out of the station. In the meantime, whenever you're ready to have your beds made, just see the porter and he'll take care of it for you."

When the conductor reached Hawke's seat, he stopped.

"Do you think we'll have any more trouble from those men?" he asked.

"No, I don't think so," Hawke replied, sighing in vexation. He had hoped to keep the entire episode from Rachel, but the conductor had just let the cat out of the bag.

"I want to know how much we appreciate what you did, Marshal. There are some pretty steep grades in the

Ozarks, and I'd hate to be going through them without brakes."

"It's not something I would want to do either," Hawke said. "And I'm glad I could be of service."

Rachel waited until the conductor left before she said anything. "Why did the conductor call you Marshal?" she asked.

"It seemed a convenient cover at the time," Hawke said.

"And what was he talking about, going through the hills without brakes. What men?" she added, piling one question on top of another. Then, suddenly, she realized what it was all about. "Oh Lord, Mason. Are you telling me there are more men out there after us?"

"Not more. It was our same two friends," Hawke said. "The ones we met earlier this evening."

The train started forward with a series of yanks and jerks before finally smoothing out. It rolled slowly at first, then began picking up speed as it left the station.

Inexplicably, Rachel laughed. "They weren't running around the yard naked, were they?" she asked.

Hawke laughed as well, glad that she was able to see some humor in the situation. "No, they had clothes on."

"Too bad. I was rather enjoying the idea of them running bare-assed around St. Louis."

Ned and Luby lay on the floor of the empty boxcar, recovering their breath after the run, both through the train shed and the final rapid sprint to catch the freight train as it was leaving the station.

"What was that son of a bitch doin' on the train?" Luby asked. "I thought they wasn't supposed to board until eight-thirty."

"They let the high-class passengers on first," Ned said. "That's so they can get all settled in them fancy cars."

The freight rolled over several switch connectors then and

beneath them the wheels clacked and the entire car shook and rattled.

"This sure as hell ain't no fancy car," Ned added.

"You ever rode in one of them fancy cars like that?" Luby asked.

"No," Ned replied. "But I expect I will, once we get this job done and them Italians pay us. I may just take me a trip and go first-class."

"Where will you go?"

"Maybe to Paducah, or New York, or Omaha, or some-place like that."

Chapter 29

"LUBY! LUBY, WAKE UP!" NED HISSED.

Luby groaned once, then opened his eyes.

Even with the side door open, it was dark in the boxcar, and Luby rubbed his eyes.

"What is it?" he asked. "What do you want?"

"We're gettin' off here."

Awake now, Luby looked through the open door. He could see tall trees whipping by, dark shadows against the star-filled sky. He could hear the sound of the engine, the roar of passing wind, the growl of wheels rolling on the track, and the squeak of the shuddering, twisting boxcar.

"What do you mean we're getting off here? Where is here?"

"Here is here," Ned said again. He started kicking Luby, not too hard, but not all that lightly either. "Come on, get up, let's go."

"Are you crazy? This is the middle of night, in the middle of nowhere, and the train is still movin'."

"You're gonna jump off with me or I'm gonna push your

ass off. One way or the other, you're getting off here," Ned said. "Now come on."

Getting up reluctantly, Luby followed Ned to the open door of the boxcar. The sound of the wind and the wheels rolling across the track was much louder here. Here too they could smell the smoke from the engine.

"Jump!" Ned shouted, pushing, even as he gave the order. The two men leaped out into the black maw of night. They hit the ground and rolled painfully for several tumbles, then stopped.

"Anything broken?" Ned asked.

"No," Luby answered after examining himself. "That ain't no thanks to you, though. What the hell did you want to jump off the train in the middle of the night, in the middle of nowhere, for? That don't make no sense a'tall."

"We've come far enough," Ned said. "I figure we had no more'n a two-hour head start comin' out of St. Louis, three at the most, so pretty soon now they'll be shuntin' us off to a sidetrack to let the passenger train pass us by. When that happens, it'll be too late."

"So, what are we going to do now? Jump on the passenger train when it comes by?"

"No, I've got a better idea," Ned said. "I was looking out the open door just before I kicked you awake, and I seen that we passed over a trestle."

"What's so important about the trestle?"

"We want to stop the train that the whore and the piano player are on, don't we?" Ned asked.

Luby laughed. "Yeah," he said. "Yeah, I get it. We knock down the trestle, they might just take a tumble."

"Maybe you ain't so dumb, after all," Ned said.

"I don't like it when you do that," Luby complained.

"You don't like it when I do what?"

"When you call me dumb, like that. I ain't dumb."

"You ain't, huh? Well, you're teamed up with me, ain't you? You can't get much dumber than to team up with me."

Luby thought about the comment for a long moment, then realized that it was a joke and he laughed. "Yeah," he said. "You can't get no dumber'n that."

The two men started walking east along the track while, behind them, the train they had just left was rapidly disappearing in the distance. The train blew its whistle and it sounded a long way off.

"Hey, Ned, how are we goin' to knock that trestle down?"

"I seen a little toolshed right there alongside it," Ned replied. "I figure we can get all the tools we need from that."

"How far back is it?"

"Can't be more'n a half a mile," Ned answered. "A mile at the most."

"A mile? Damn, that's a long walk in the dark," Luby said.

"Stay on the track, you won't get lost," Ned said.

"I wasn't worried about gettin' lost. I was just commentin', that's all."

It took them about twenty minutes to reach the trestle, and by then the eastern horizon was streaked with red and pink. It would be full light within half an hour.

"It's goin' to be mornin' soon," Luby said.

"That's good," Ned said. "Come mornin', we'll have enough light to work by. The only question now is: Will the train get there before we get finished?"

"You think it might?"

"If we don't quit gabbin', it might."

They walked across the trestle, stepping carefully on each of the cross ties.

"There's the toolshed I was tellin' you about," Ned said, pointing to a small wood building just off the track.

"Damn, the shed's got a lock on it," Luby said, pointing to the door.

Ned pulled his gun and aimed it at the lock. The gun boomed, the bullet tore through the body of the lock, and the hasp popped open.

"Now it don't," he said with a satisfied grunt.

"What kind of tools do you reckon we'll need?"

"Crowbars and sledgehammers, I reckon," Ned said. "We're going to take a section of track right out of the middle, then knock over the timbers. That ought to be enough to stop them."

Luby pulled out the tools and the two men started working. They sweated and grunted for a few minutes, then Luby laughed.

"What is it?"

"I always swore I'd never do hard work," he said. "Now look at me. I'm slaving away here as hard as any gandy dancer you ever seen."

"You ever knowed a gandy dancer who got a thousand dollars for about half an hour's work on the railroad?"

"No."

"Well, that's what you're gettin'."

"Ha!" Luby said as he swung the sledgehammer. "I didn't think of it like that."

Hawke and Rachel were having breakfast in the dining car when the engineer suddenly applied his brakes, causing the train to brake so hard that the breakfast dishes slid off the table. A steward was just delivering the meal to one of the other tables when the hard braking action started, which caused him to fall, sending the contents of his tray crashing to the floor.

A couple of the women diners cried out in alarm and one of the male passengers cursed in anger.

With a squealing, sliding, shuddering sound, the train finally came to a complete stop.

"Oh, what is it? What's happening?" Rachel asked.

"My guess is something on the track," Hawke said. "Let me check on it."

Leaving the dining car, Hawke stepped down onto the ballast-covered ground alongside the train, then hurried forward to the engine. Though sitting still, the engine was alive with potential energy . . . spitting steam and percolating water as if protesting the indignity of having been forced to stop while at full speed. Others were beginning to get off the train as well, and Hawke could hear them calling out to each other in curiosity, wondering what was wrong and why the train had made such an abrupt stop.

The engineer and fireman were standing at the front of the engine when Hawke arrived.

"Mr. Hawke, didn't you say you was the U.S. Marshal?" the engineer asked.

For a second Hawke didn't know what the engineer was talking about, then he remembered that he had made that claim when he was chasing Ned and Luby.

"Uh, yeah," Hawke replied. "Actually, I'm a deputy U.S. Marshal."

Again, he hoped he wouldn't be asked to produce any proof.

"Well, sir, there's somethin' queer about this, and I was wonderin' if you wouldn't mind comin' down with me to have a look?"

"I'd be glad to," Hawke said, pleased that he was being asked to have a look around, rather than being put in the position of having to ask.

Hawke and Charley walked to the front of the train, then down the track several feet until they reached the edge of the trestle. It wasn't a very long trestle, as the gully the little bridge spanned was barely over twenty feet long and no more than ten feet deep.

Not all the trestle was down. There was a section about twelve feet long, missing from the exact middle.

"It's a lucky thing you saw this," Hawke said.

"I know. The track makes a little curve back there and I just happened to be lookin' in the right direction to catch it," Charley answered. "Nine times out of ten, I wouldn't have happened to glance over like that, and I wouldn't have seen it in time to stop."

The two men walked out onto the trestle itself and stood at the very edge of the break.

"Marshal, this here ain't no accident," the engineer said. "Looks to me like someone pulled up the track, then knocked over the timbers that supported it. The rails and timbers are still here. See 'em down there?"

"Yeah, I see them," Hawke replied.

"We could'a run right off of this thing," the engineer said. "And, goin' as fast as we was, we would'a busted the boiler wide open. Me 'n Wayne would be dead for sure, and like as not, a lot of other folks as well."

Hawke put his hand on Charley's shoulder. "It's a good thing for all of us that you are as careful as you are."

"Yes, sir, well, I've always tried to be," Charley replied.

By now most of the rest of the crew and passengers had reached the front end of the train and they stood there, staring at the missing section of trestle.

"Have you ever run into anything like this before?" Hawke asked.

"No, sir. Well, not deliberate, that is. But I've come across down bridges and track outages."

"What do you do about it?" Hawke asked.

"Well, first thing we have to do is put up warnin' flags behind us, and then some on the other side of the trestle. That'll keep any other trains from runnin' into us or off the track. Then we'll have to send someone on ahead to Sedalia and get a work crew out here."

"How far is it to Sedalia?"

"I'd say about five miles."

"That's an hour and a half at a brisk walk," Hawke suggested.

The engineer smiled. "Not if Lorenzo goes."

"Lorenzo?"

"Lorenzo's one of our porters," Charley said. "He's one of them fellas that likes to run—and not just a little ways. He likes to run a long ways. He's always doin' it. If we turn him loose, he could get to Sedalia in forty minutes . . . say twenty minutes to get a work crew back here and half an hour more to put the track back in place. We'll be on our way in no time." The engineer turned to yell at his fireman. "Wayne! Wayne, have Lorenzo come up!"

A few minutes later a slender young black man came up to the front of the train. Charley explained what was needed and Lorenzo nodded, then reached down and retied both shoes. That done, he started up the track at a brisk pace.

A shot rang out, and Lorenzo tumbled down the side of the track berm.

"Lorenzo!" Charley shouted, and he started toward the porter.

"I'm all right, Mr. Charley. Don't come here!" Lorenzo shouted back. "I'm just stayin' out of the way of whoever's shootin' at me!"

Another shot rang out and this time the passengers, amid screams and shouts, started running pell-mell.

Most ran away from the shooting, but Hawke, having seen where the puff of smoke came from, started running toward it.

The third shot was fired directly at Hawke and it came close enough for him to hear the angry buzz of the bullet.

By now, Hawke had his pistol in his hand and he dived into the dirt behind a poison sumac bush just as another bullet cut through the leaves.

"Uhnn," Hawke yelled, then he lay perfectly still.

"Hey, Ned! Ned, I think I got 'im!" a voice called excitedly.

"Go check 'im out. See if he's dead," Ned replied.

"All right, I . . . wait a minute! I ain't goin' to check 'im out. You check 'im out."

"You're the one says you shot 'im!"

It was Ned and Luby! How did they get here, to the trestle, before the train did?

Hawke didn't move. After a few moments, he heard the sound of boots on rocks as someone came walking up the dry ravine toward him.

"He ain't movin'," Luby said. Now Luby's voice was very close. "I think I got 'im."

"Make sure the son of a bitch is dead, then let's go kill the whore," Ned called back.

Hawke waited until Luby was right over him, then he turned over.

"What the hell?" Luby gasped, bringing his pistol up.

Hawke pulled the trigger and his bullet hit Luby under the chin. Luby fell back.

"Luby, what happened?" Ned called. When he didn't get an answer, he called again. "Luby, is he dead? Did you kill 'im?"

Hawke crawled on his belly, away from the poison sumac, over to a growth of wild berries.

"Luby?"

Hawke saw Ned stand up.

"Luby's dead, Ned!" Hawke called.

Ned swung around toward the sound of Hawke's voice and

started firing wildly. His gun boomed three times. Hawke shot back, only once, but once was enough. His bullet found its mark and Ned threw up his gun and fell over backward. Hawke ran over to the fallen outlaw and knelt beside him. He could see bubbles of blood coming from Ned's mouth. Ned was trying hard to breathe, and Hawke heard a sucking sound in his chest. He knew that his bullet had punctured Ned's lungs.

"Why did you come after us?" Hawke asked. "You aren't Mafia, are you?"

"Mafia?" Ned tried to cough, and as he did so, he sprayed blood. "Who is Mafia?"

"How did you know how to find us?" Hawke asked.

"Bellefont."

"What?"

"Belle . . ." Ned started to say, then he drew in two short, audible gasps before he stopped breathing.

"Ned?" Hawke said, shaking him gently. "Ned?"

Ned didn't respond, and Hawke put his hand to his neck. Ned was dead.

When Hawke got back to the train, only the engineer, fireman, conductor, and Lorenzo were still standing outside. The others had all retreated back to the train when the shooting started.

"Did you get them?" Charley asked.

"Yeah," Hawke said, nodding.

"Wonder what they wanted to rob this train for? We aren't carrying anything," Bates said.

"You think I can start into town now, Mr. Bates?" Lorenzo asked.

"What do you think, Mr. Hawke?" the conductor asked.

"Yes. You can go now. They're both dead."

Lorenzo looked at the engineer.

"Go on, Lorenzo, get started," Charley said. "Otherwise we'll be out here all day."

Lorenzo nodded, then started running. Within a minute he was already out of sight.

Chapter 30

EVERYONE ELSE ONBOARD THE TRAIN THOUGHT IT was a failed train robbery attempt, but Rachel knew better.

"It was Tangeleno, wasn't it?" she asked, when Hawke returned to the train.

"Yeah," Hawke said. "It was the same two we ran into back in St. Louis."

"How did they get here, ahead of us?"

"They probably took an earlier train, then got off and waited for us," Hawke said. "The real question is: How do they know about Bellefont?"

"Bellefont? They don't know about Bellefont. Nobody knows about Bellefont. I didn't make up my mind that I was going there myself until just before I left New Orleans. And I didn't tell anyone."

"Just before he died, the one named Ned said Bellefont."

Rachel shook her head. "I swear to you, Mason, I never told a soul until I told you. I don't have any idea how he could have possibly known that I am going to Bellefont."

"You said you didn't make the decision to go to Bellefont until just before you left."

"That's right."

"Why Bellefont? Why not Dodge City? Ft. Worth? Tucson? What made you choose Bellefont?"

"I told you, I'm going to buy a gambling house there."

"How did you know about the gambling house?"

"I have a friend who lives there. We've been exchanging letters for the past year. She told me about it."

"Did you keep those letters?"

"Yes, of course I did. She is a very good friend, and the letters are dear to me."

"Did you bring them with you?"

"No. After the shooting, I was afraid to go back to the house."

"So your letters are still back in your room," Hawke said. It was a statement, not a question.

"Yes."

"That's how they learned about Bellefont. They found your letters."

"But how could they? Clarisse would never let anyone into my . . ." Rachel gasped and put her hand to her mouth. "Oh, Mason, you don't think they hurt Clarisse, do you?"

"They may not have hurt her," Hawke said. "But if they wanted to get into your room, there is no way she could have stopped them."

Less than two hours after Lorenzo left, he and a work team returned on a handcar. Lorenzo went from car to car, beaming broadly as he received his just praise for getting a work crew back in such a timely fashion.

The work crew was fast and efficient and, within forty-five minutes after they arrived, the track was repaired and the *Kansas City Flyer* was under way once more.

When the train made a sudden and unscheduled stop that morning, Dallipiccola thought that opportunity had come for him to take care of his business with the piano player and the whore. But when practically everyone on the train went outside to see what was going on, he realized that he would have to wait a little longer.

He was as surprised as everyone else when a gun battle broke out between Hawke and a couple of unseen assailants. And, like the others, he initially thought it was a botched train robbery. But when the two bodies were brought up and displayed to the morbidly curious, he was surprised to see that it was Ned and Luby.

Back in Bellefont, Vizzini went into the telegraph office and stepped up to the counter. A sign hanging over the counter read: BUFORD RODMAN—TELEGRAPHER. And, as it so happened, Rodman was getting a telegram at that very moment.

"I'll be right with you, sir," he said, looking up. He continued to transcribe the telegram, then, smiling, he brushed his hands together and walked up to the counter. "Yes, sir, what can I do for you?"

"Have you got any telegrams for Mrs. Louise Smalley?" Vizzini asked.

Rodman looked surprised. "Yes, as a matter of fact, one just came in for her."

"Let me have it. I'll take it to her," Vizzini offered.

The telegrapher looked surprised by the offer. "Well, I don't know. I'm not supposed to entrust the telegram to anyone but the recipient."

"You mean you don't use telegraph delivery boys?"

"Well yes, I have Jimmy, when he's here," Rodman said. He looked around the office. "But I have to admit that he isn't very responsible, though. More than half the time I have to either go look him up or deliver the telegram myself."

"If you want to deliver it yourself, that's fine with me," Vizzini said. "It's just that Louise asked me to pick it up for her."

"Louise?"

"She is my sister," Vizzini said. "I'm in town visiting her."

Rodman smiled broadly. "Well, sir, if you are Mrs. Smalley's brother, then I see no reason why I shouldn't give you the message." He tore the message off the pad, then stuck it down into an envelope and handed it to Vizzini. "I appreciate it."

"You're welcome," Vizzini said.

With the telegram in hand, Vizzini returned to the hotel.

"You were right," he said, handing the telegram to Tangeleno. "She did get one."

"Yeah, I figured she would," Tangeleno said, reaching for the envelope.

"Let's see what it says."

I Will Be Arriving On the 7th Instant Stop Rachel

"They'll be here tomorrow," Tangeleno said, handing the message to Vizzini. "Did you have any trouble getting it?"

"No. I just told him I was her brother."

"Good, good," Tangeleno said. "Come on, let's go get a drink," he offered.

When Tangeleno and Vizzini went into the Brown Dirt a few minutes later, the bartender called out to him.

"Mr. Tangeleno," he said. "I got somethin' here I think you might like."

Looking toward the bar, Tangeleno saw that the bartender was holding up a bottle of Chianti.

"Turns out that Mr. Algood had a bottle 'n' he sold it to me," he said.

"That's very good of you," Tangeleno said. "Oh, this is my friend, Mr. Vizzini."

"Vizzini, huh?" Ely said. "Well, I'll say this, Mr. Vizzini. Any friend of Mr. Tangeleno's is certainly welcome in my bar."

"Actually," Vizzini said. "Any friend of Mr. Tangeleno's is welcome anywhere."

Ely tried to pull the cork on the wine bottle, but couldn't get it out. He started to use his teeth.

"Here, don't do that," Tangeleno said. Don't you have a corkscrew?"

Ely looked confused. "I don't know what that is," he said.

"Never mind, I'll take care of it." Tangeleno said. Pulling up his trouser leg, he took a knife from a sheath that was strapped to his ankle. He sliced off the top half of the cork, then pushed the bottom half down into the bottle.

"I'll say this for you," Ely said. "You seem to keep knives and guns all over the place."

"Get us some glasses," Tangeleno ordered.

Ely started to reach for a glass.

"Clean glasses," Tangeleno said.

"Yes, sir."

Tangeleno poured himself a glass of wine, then handed the bottle to Vizzini. Vizzini poured his own wine, then resealed the bottle with the top half of the cork. He didn't make any effort to pay for the wine, and Ely didn't ask.

Tangeleno and Vizzini took their glasses of wine with them and walked over to one of the tables.

Everyone in town feared Tangeleno now. It wasn't just the fact that he had killed both Deekus and Farley, it was the absolute cold calmness of his demeanor afterward. One person described looking into Tangeleno's eyes as "gazing into the portals of hell."

"Damn me if that new feller don't look near as bad as Tangeleno," one of the men said quietly. "You reckon he carries him a gun under his jacket too?"

"From the looks of things, I'd say more'n one gun. And maybe two or three knives to boot," Ely replied.

"Why do you reckon they carry their guns under their jacket?"

"Why not?" Ely asked. "I reckon he can carry it about anywhere he wants to carry it."

"Well, come on, you can't make no fast draw from there."

" 'Fast draw'?" Ely said, laughing dryly. "Fast draw is for folks who make a game of killin'. If you take a good look at these two fellers, killin' ain't no game. For them it's all business."

"What do you think they are doin' in Bellefont, anyway?"

"I don't know," Ely answered. "But I hope they don't stay long."

Back on the train, Dallipiccola waited all day and into the night, looking for the perfect opportunity to kill Hawke and Rachel. Then, at midnight, when he was certain that nearly everyone on the train was asleep, he left his car to go find them. He would kill them both quietly, in the middle of the night, then he would leave the train and be halfway back to St. Louis before the bodies were even discovered.

The porters kept the train cars dark, in order to provide a relaxing atmosphere for the passengers. With only low-burning gimbals mounted lanterns at the front and rear walls kept the cars dark so the passengers could sleep. The day cars were the easiest to check, because all the seats were exposed and filled with passengers, twisted in tortured positions in an attempt to get comfortable.

The two sleeper cars were more difficult to check because all the berths were behind curtains. There were porters in each of the sleeper cars, but, like their passengers, they were asleep. The porters were sitting on a small stool at the back end of their respective cars, leaning against the wall, moving slightly with the sway of the train.

When Dallipiccola opened the first curtain, he realized, to his frustration, that it was too dark to see anything. He was about to give up, when he saw a candle lying on the bed. Evidently before the passenger had gone to sleep, he had been reading by candlelight.

Dallipiccola carried the candle down to the lantern, lit it, and then used it to illuminate the berths. He initially planned to examine every berth, but then reasoned that if he found one of them in the top berth, the other one would surely be in the bottom.

That reasoning enabled him to get through both sleeper cars more quickly than he thought he would. But it also proved to be a fruitless search, because he didn't see either one of them.

Finally, he came to the Palace Car. Since he had already checked all the other cars, he knew this was where they had to be.

Dallipiccola stepped across the vestibule connector plates, but found that the door to the Palace Car was locked. He tried to open it but was startled when it was jerked opened from the inside. A porter stood just inside the door, blocking the way.

"Yes, sir, what can I do for you?" the porter asked.

"I, uh, just want to see what a fancy car like this looks like inside," he said.

"I'm sorry, sir, but I can't let you in."

"Why not? I won't bother anyone."

"Because that's the rules," the porter said, as if that were all the reason he needed.

For just a moment, Dallipiccola considered trying to bribe his way in, but decided that it might make him too memorable. And in his business, it wasn't good to be too memorable.

"I understand. I'm sorry if I bothered you," Dallipiccola said.

"Ain't no bother, sir," the porter said. "We gets folks all the time wantin' to take a look inside. But, like I say, I can't let you in."

"You are a good man," Dallipiccola said as, without argument, he returned to his seat. He had taken passage in one of the day cars, and he cursed himself now for his parsimoniousness as he settled in as best he could to spend an uncomfortable night. He was a patient man, and he was certain that if he waited, opportunity would present itself.

Chapter 31

~~~~~

THE NEXT MORNING AN IMPROMPTU RACE BROKE out between a coyote and the *Kansas City Flyer*. The coyote kept pace with it for a while, but finally broke off its chase as the huge engine, with wisps of steam streaming back from the driver wheels, pounded tirelessly down the long lonesome expanse of railroad track.

Inside the train Hawke and Rachel had just returned from breakfast and were sitting in the elegant lounge area in the middle of the Palace Car. The big, comfortable, overstuffed chairs would rotate so passengers could either watch the scenery roll by just outside the window or turn their chairs inward so they could engage in conversation with their fellow passengers. The walls were richly paneled with rosewood and the floor was carpeted to deaden the noise of the undercarriage. On a table near the porter's station, there were containers of coffee, tea, and water.

Rachel had her chair facing the window, watching the scenery, when she realized that they were traveling much faster than they had been.

"My," Rachel said. "Look how fast the ground is going by. We must be going very fast."

"We are indeed," the conductor said, looking back toward Rachel. "We are doing better than forty miles an hour now, trying to make up for lost time."

"Forty miles per hour? I don't think I've ever gone that fast," Rachel said. She turned to look out the window again, then she gasped. "Mason!"

"What is it?" Hawke asked.

Rachel pointed out the window at the shadow of the train as it slid quickly along the ground.

"The shadow," she said. "I saw his shadow!"

"You saw whose shadow?"

"I don't know. Some man," Rachel said. "He is on the roof of the train."

"Where is he? On this car?" Hawke asked.

"No, when I saw him, he was a few cars up that way," Rachel said, pointing forward. "I can't see him right now, but a moment ago there was an open area and I could see the shadow of the entire train."

"Mr. Bates," Hawke said, calling to the conductor, who had moved to the back of the car. "Do we have brakemen on top of this train?"

"Brakemen? Oh no, we don't use brakemen on our passenger trains now. We have air brakes. Why?"

"We thought we saw the shadow of someone on top of the train."

Bates laughed and shook his head. "Oh, I hardly think that. It must've been an optical illusion of some sort. Why, who would walk on top of this train at forty miles per hour?"

"He wasn't walking, actually. He was all crouched over, and he was running along the top," Rachel said.

"Which way was he heading?" Hawke asked, leaning over

to peer through the window. "Was he going toward the front of the train or toward the rear?"

"Toward the rear," Rachel answered.

"Mr. Hawke, surely you don't think she actually saw someone up there, do you?" Bates asked.

"Yes, I think she may have," he said.

"What on earth would make you think such a thing?"

"Mafia," Hawke said.

Rachel reached out to squeeze Hawke's hand. "Oh," she said.

"Mafia? What is Mafia? Is that a man's name?"

"I think I'll check it out," Hawke said.

Hawke started toward the back door of the car, hooking the strap over his pistol to keep it from falling out.

"Mr. Hawke, where do you think you are going?" the conductor asked as Hawke reached for the door.

"I'm going up there to take a look around."

"No, sir, I'm sorry, but I can't allow you to do that," Bates said.

"Mr. Bates, they cut the brake hose in St. Louis. And you said yourself that if we hadn't discovered that, it could have caused a wreck," Hawke said. "Those same two men took out a trestle this morning. If the engineer had not seen it in time, that would have wrecked the train. Now, it would appear there is someone else on top of the train, and you say it isn't a brakeman. So, do you really want to take a chance that it is just an optical illusion?"

"No, I . . . I suppose not," Bates said. "Do what you feel you must do, but, I must caution you, the Missouri Pacific takes no responsibility for anything that might happen to you."

"Don't worry. I won't blame the Missouri Pacific," Hawke said.

Hawke stepped through the back door of the car. This was the last car, so the back vestibule was open. As he stood there, he could see the track unwinding so quickly behind him that the cross ties were a complete blur.

The ground was whipping by at such a speed that he grew dizzy. He didn't even like being out here at this speed, let alone up on top of the car. But he figured if someone else could do it, he could do it too.

Taking a deep breath of resolve, Hawke grabbed the little access ladder, then climbed to the top. He crawled out onto the roof of the car and lay there for a moment until he got his balance. There was a pendulum effect in the sway of the cars, with the wheels being the attaching point and the top of the car being the outer end of the pendulum arm. That meant that, up here, the swaying of the car was much more pronounced. Also, the blast of air, which, on the vestibule platform, was normally diverted by the car, was very strong up here. It was going to be difficult just to keep from falling off. Hawke stayed on his hands and knees for a moment until he was sure of his balance, then he stood up and looked toward the front of the train.

About two cars in front of him, he saw a man rise up. The man saw Hawke at the same time.

"What are you doing up here?" Hawke shouted, even though he knew he probably couldn't be heard. His words sounded thin in the rush of wind and the roar of the train.

Dallipiccola fired at Hawke, then he turned and started running away from him, back toward the front of the train. Hawke dropped down to the roof of the car and fired back, but he missed. Dallipiccola also dropped down, then scooted forward on his belly until he reached the front of the car. He scrambled over, then climbed down. Hawke got up and started running toward him.

Suddenly Dallipiccola appeared again, this time shielded by the car so that only his head could be seen. Raising his pistol over the edge of the car, he fired, and the bullet clipped

the roof just in front of Hawke. Hawke returned fire and saw
a shower of sparks made by his own bullet as it disintegrated
against the top of the ladder to which Dallipiccola was cling-
ing.

Down in the engine cab, the noise prevented Charley and
Wayne from hearing the firing, so they were unaware of the
drama being played out behind them. Their task was to coax
as much speed as possible from the locomotive and they
were doing just that. Charley was keeping the throttle wide-
open, while Wayne shoveled in coal with the regularity of a
machine. The train was thundering down the track and whipping around a large-radius curve at a tremendous speed.

As the train started around the curve, it opened the gap between the cars just enough for Hawke to take a well-aimed
shot. But when Hawke pulled the trigger, the hammer fell
upon an empty chamber. Frustrated, Hawke pulled the trigger a second time, but with the same result. He had forgotten
to reload after his engagement with Ned and Luby!

Dallipiccola realized at once that Hawke was out of bullets. Smiling, he climbed back up onto the car and started
running toward Hawke, holding his pistol extended in front
of him. He leaped across the gap between the cars, reaching
Hawke before Hawke had the opportunity to reload.

"For a piano player, you've been a very hard man to kill,"
Dallipiccola said. He laughed, then raised his pistol.

Hawke saw that the train was about to pass under a small
bridge. He saw, also, that Dallipiccola was pulling the hammer back on his pistol. "Say your prayers, Piano Player!"

"If you kill me, you'll never find the gold," Hawke shouted
back at him.

Dallipiccola got a confused look on his face. " 'Gold'?
What gold?"

"What gold? Why do you think Tangeleno has hired everyone in America to kill us? Because we got away with the gold."

There was no gold, of course. Hawke was making a desperate play for time, hoping he could hold Dallipiccola's interest just long enough. He didn't need too much time. The engine was almost to the bridge now.

As Hawke hoped he would, the man lowered the pistol. "Tangeleno didn't say anything about gold," he said.

"How'd you find out about us? By telegram?"

His assailant nodded.

Hawke chuckled. "Come on, you think he's going to put in a telegram that we stole half a million dollars in gold bars?"

The nose of the engine was passing under the bridge. There was about one second left.

"Look out behind you!" Hawke called, suddenly dropping flat on his stomach.

"You think I'm going to . . . *unhh!*"

Dallipiccola's head, traveling at forty miles per hour, smacked hard into the side of the bridge. Hawke saw a little misty spray of blood fly, then Dallipiccola was gone over the side of the train. Hawke pressed himself flat on the top of the car as the bridge passed by overhead, then he stood up and looked back at Dallipiccola's body, now lying grotesquely twisted on the track behind them.

Gingerly, he worked his way back to the end of the train, then climbed down the ladder. He stood out on the vestibule for a moment, then went back inside.

Chapter 32

AT ABOUT THAT SAME TIME, BACK IN BELLEFONT, Eddie Smalley took a last swallow of his coffee, then got up from the breakfast table. He walked around the table to kiss Louise.

"I'm going to open the store."

"Why so early? We've got another half hour before we have to open," she said. "I just heard Kathy ringing the school bell."

"Ely wanted to come in early this morning so he could get some things for the kitchen over at the Brown Dirt. He's a good customer. I like to keep him happy."

"I know. All right, you go open the store. I'll get over there as soon as I get the breakfast dishes washed."

"You don't have to hurry."

"I don't mind."

"Louise, have I ever told you how lucky I am to have you for a wife?"

"No, Eddie," she said. "I'm the lucky one. Not many men would treat me the way you have, knowing where they found me."

"Yes, well, you never know where gold is going to turn up," Eddie said with a chuckle.

Louise walked to the front door with him and kissed him again before he left. She watched him start across the street, then sighed in contentment. As Clarisse had told her before she left New Orleans, "Honey, you are about to realize every whore's dream." Turning away from the door, she returned to the kitchen to begin cleaning up.

She had just finished the dishes when she heard someone knocking at the back door. Chuckling, she started toward it.

"What did you do, Eddie, forget your key again? You should tie a . . ." she stopped in midsentence when she opened the door and saw Vizzini standing on her back porch. Vizzini was holding a shotgun.

"Vizzini!" she gasped.

Vizzini smiled an evil, ugly smile.

"I'm flattered that you remember me," he said.

"You aren't an easy man to forget," Louise said.

Vizzini reached out and let the fingers of his left hand trail across her breast. "You and I never experienced the bed of pleasure, did we?" he asked. "We should have. I'm told by those who did go up to your room with you that you were a real joy."

"What do you want?" Louise asked. "I'm not in that business anymore," she added coldly.

"Don Tangeleno wants to see you."

"Well, you just go back and tell your boss that I don't want to see him."

"If you remember, Don Tangeleno is not a man you want to disappoint," Vizzini said.

"What are you two doing here, anyway? This isn't New Orleans. There can't possibly be anything here that would interest either one of you."

"We have some business to do here, and you are going to help us."

"I'm not going to help you do anything."

"Oh, I think you will," Vizzini said. "Because if you don't, I will blow your head off with this shotgun. Then I will go into the store across the street and I will blow your husband's head off."

Louise didn't respond.

"You know me, Louise," Vizzini said. "You know Tangeleno and you know the Family. You know too that I will do as I say, don't you?"

"Yes," Louise said in a small quiet voice.

"So you will help us. Yes?"

"Yes," Louise answered, her voice so quiet now that it could barely be heard.

"Was that a yes?" Vizzini jabbed the twin barrels of the shotgun under Louise's chin, pushing it up so hard that it hurt.

"Yes," Louise said again.

"I thought so. Come along. We have things to do."

Miss Betty O'Hare had eleven students in her school. They ranged in age from six to sixteen. Right now she had her older children doing work at their seats while she was going over a reading assignment with her younger students. When, unexpectedly, the door opened, she looked up to see Louise coming in.

"Why, Mrs. Smalley, what a pleasant surprise," Betty said. "What brings you here for a visit?"

Two men stepped into the school behind Louise and Betty saw that they were both carrying shotguns.

"What is this? What's going on?" Betty asked in alarm.

"That one," Tangeleno said, pointing to one of the students.

Vizzini walked over and grabbed the student Tangeleno had pointed out, a young girl of about twelve.

"Miss O'Hare!" the young girl called out.

"Don't make another sound, girl," Vizzini said. "If you do, I'll pull the trigger."

The girl began crying, though her sobs were subdued.

"Get your students all together, teacher," Tangeleno said. "We're all going to church."

" 'Church'? I don't understand," Betty said.

"You don't have to understand. All you have to do is do what I say. Get all these kids rounded up, take them through the back door of the school, across the schoolyard, and into the back door of the church."

"I will do no such thing."

"Then we will kill this girl to show you that we are serious," Tangeleno said. He looked toward Vizzini. "Do it," he ordered.

Vizzini pulled the hammer back on one of the barrels of his shotgun.

"Betty, for God's sake, do it!" Louise said desperately. "I know these men! Vizzini will do exactly what Tangeleno tells him to do!"

Betty hesitated for just a second, then she said, "All right, children, let's do what the men say. Out the back door, across the yard, and into the church."

"I want my mama," one very young girl whimpered.

"Don't worry, *piccolo uno*, you will see your mama very soon," Tangeleno said. "Oh, and let me warn you, if anyone tries to run, we will kill this girl."

"Don't anyone run," Betty said. "Please, don't anyone run."

The church was right next door to the school and the little group of students and adults crossed the yard, then went in through the back door of the church. The reverend was sitting at his desk writing when they all came in.

"Well," he said, smiling broadly. "Have you come to have a . . ." He stopped in midsentence when he saw the two men with shotguns, one of which was pressed to a young girl's head. "What is this?" he asked.

"The sign out front says your name is Reverend Timothy Gadbury," Tangeleno said.

"I am."

"Well, Reverend Gadbury, my name is Joseph Tangeleno. I'm sure you haven't heard of me, but—"

"I've heard of you, Mr. Tangeleno," Gadbury said. "I conducted the funerals for Deekus and Farley Carter."

"Good, then you realize that we are people who deserve respect."

"Io non ho rispetto per un assassino," Gadbury said in clipped angry tones.

"You have no respect for a murderer? Bravo, bravo, Padre. I didn't know you spoke Italian."

"What do you want, Tangeleno?"

"I want to borrow your church."

"It isn't my church. It is God's church."

"Madre di Dio," Tangeleno said, sighing and throwing up his hand. "All right, then I want to borrow God's church. I'm sure He won't mind."

"Why do you want to borrow the church?"

"Because it is the only place large enough to hold every man, woman, and child in town."

"I don't understand," Gadbury said.

"It isn't important that you understand. It is only important that you get everyone to come to the church. Everyone," he said with emphasis.

"How do you expect me to do that? On the best Sunday just over half the people in the town come to church."

"You are going to tell them that if everyone is not in this church, one hour from now, I am going to start killing the schoolchildren. And I will kill one of them every five minutes until I have killed all of them—or until everyone in town is in this church."

"You are mad!" Gadbury said.

"No, Padre, I am determined," Tangeleno said. "And the hour starts now," he said, looking at his pocket watch. "Oh, I will send Louise with you to help you round everyone up."

Gadbury continued to stare angrily at Tangeleno.

"You had better get going, Reverend," Vizzini said. "Don Tangeleno don't like to be kept waiting." Vizzini looked at his watch. "And two minutes have already passed. What if the last person doesn't get here until two minutes too late, and I have already killed this girl?" He jabbed the shotgun against the young girl's neck and she whimpered.

"That would be the two minutes that you have already wasted. Wouldn't you feel bad about being the cause of that?"

"Come, Mrs. Smalley," Gadbury said, starting toward the front door of the church. "We must make haste."

Vizzini laughed. "'Make haste,'" he said. "Yeah, I like that. What is that? Some sort of sermon talk?"

Gadbury glared at Vizzini. "Do no harm to the children," he said as he and Louise left.

Within minutes after Gadbury left, the first of the townspeople started coming in. Tangeleno met them at the door. One of the men, standing just in front of the marquee, was wearing a pistol belt.

"Leave your gun outside," Tangeleno ordered.

"The hell I will! You let those children go!" the man shouted, making a grab for his pistol.

Tangeleno whirled his shotgun around and pulled the trigger while the man was still bringing his pistol up. The blast caught him in the upper chest, neck, and face, and slammed him back against the church marquee. He slid down, gasped a few times for breath, then died. From inside the church, the children screamed, and Tangeleno turned his gun toward them.

"Be quiet!" he ordered. "I will shoot the next person who screams."

There were no more incidents after that and, within an hour, the church was filled.

"Is this everyone, Louise?" Tangeleno asked when she and the preacher returned. Louise's husband was with her.

"Yes, this is everyone."

Tangeleno looked over the church for a moment, then nodded. "You know, Louise, I believe you are right. Even Ely and the whores who work for him are here."

Ely, Maggie, and Sally, the other "soiled dove," were sitting near the back.

"Tell me, Padre, is this the first time you've ever had a whore in your church?" Tangeleno asked.

Gadbury didn't answer.

"Ah, no, wait. Louise is one of your regulars, isn't she?"

"Mrs. Smalley attends church quite regularly, yes," Gadbury replied.

"Well, then, this is not the first time you've had a whore in your church, is it?"

"I don't know what you are talking about," the preacher said.

"Of course you don't. So, Louise, is this your husband?"

Louise didn't answer.

"I think he is your husband. I can tell by the way he looks at you. Mr. Smalley, did you know that before she came here, your wife was a whore? I am told she was quite good. I can't speak for myself, of course; she never spread her legs for me. But my friends have told me she was very good. What about it, Mr. Smalley? Is she very good?"

"Why, you low-assed, piss-complexioned, maggot-infested, pig-faced son of a bitch!" Eddie said, starting toward him.

Tangeleno pointed his shotgun at the kids and he pulled the hammer back. "Take one more step and I'll pull the trigger," he said. "With this scattergun I'll kill at least two of them and hurt a lot more. Do you want to see that?"

Eddie glared at him.

"Eddie, no," Louise said. "It's not worth it."

Looking around the room, Eddie saw that several of the townspeople were looking on in shock over what they had just heard.

"It's true," Eddie said. "I met her in New Orleans. I knew what she was when I met her, but I didn't care. I fell in love with her."

"Oh," Tangeleno said. "Did I give away your secret?"

"We love her as well," Gadbury said. "The entire town loves her."

"Yes, but that was before you knew she was a whore," Tangeleno said. "What do you think of her now?"

"Even Jesus forgave the prostitutes," Gadbury said. "I don't know who or what she was in New Orleans, but here, I am proud to say that she is Mrs. Smalley, a member of our church and my friend."

"My friend too," Betty said and immediately the others, including Maggie and Sally, gathered around Louise to extend their assurances that nothing had changed.

Tangeleno clapped quietly. "What a tender scene," he said. "I am impressed by the goodness of the people in this town."

"Coming out of your mouth, Tangeleno, even the word 'goodness' has a foulness to it," Gadbury said.

"I'll say this for you, Padre. You've got sand," Tangeleno said. Then to Louise he said, "Oh, I almost forgot. I have a telegram for you."

"You . . . have a telegram for me?"

"It's my fault, Mrs. Smalley," Rodman said. "That other man with the shotgun was there when the telegram came in yesterday. He told me he was your brother, so I gave it to him."

"I'm sorry I'm late in telling you about it," Tangeleno said. "Suppose I just read it to you?" Without waiting for a response, Tangeleno took the message out of his pocket and read it. " 'I will be arriving on the 7th. Instant. Stop. Rachel.' "

Tangeleno looked up at her. "That is right, isn't it? You are expecting your friend Rachel to come to Bellefont today?"

"Yes," Louise said.

"Good. Now you folks just relax and make yourselves comfortable. This will all be over by this afternoon."

"What do you mean everything will be over this afternoon?" Louise asked.

"It will be over as soon as I kill Rachel and the man she is traveling with," Tangeleno said.

Chapter 33

ALTHOUGH THE SUN WAS LOW IN THE WESTERN sky, there was still quite a bit of light when the train reached Bellefont. There were no departing passengers waiting at the station, and no one who was just curious to see the train as it arrived. As a result, Hawke and Rachel, who were the only two arriving passengers, stepped out onto a deserted platform in a very quiet town.

The door to the baggage car opened and the baggage handler stood there looking out.

"Matt!" he called. "Matt, we got luggage!"

The conductor left the train as well, and he flipped open his watch to check the time.

"That's funny. It's not like Matt to miss a train," he said. "Come to think of it, this time of day, there's normally a dozen or so people here. I wonder where everyone is."

"Has this ever happened before?" Hawke asked. "I mean for you to arrive and there be absolutely no one to meet the train."

"Oh, it has from time to time," the conductor said. "Like if there is somethin' goin' on in town . . . a wedding or something. But normally there is someone here . . . at least to handle the baggage."

"Why don't I just walk down to the baggage car and have the luggage handed down to me?" Hawke asked.

The conductor chuckled. "If you're going to get your luggage, looks like that's the only way it's going to happen."

"Oh, would you mind taking this as well?" The baggage handler asked after he had handed down Hawke and Rachel's luggage. He was holding a small canvas pouch.

"What is this?" Hawke asked.

"According to the bill of lading, it's a knife. Anyway, it is to be left with the hotel clerk. A man named Cassius Cole will pick it up sometime next week. All the information is in a letter just inside the pouch."

"All right. Give it to me," Hawke said. "If I can't find the station master, I'll take it over to the hotel myself."

"Thanks, I appreciate that," the baggage clerk said as he handed the bag down to Hawke. He closed the door to the car and Hawke carried the two pieces of luggage and the canvas bag over to where Rachel and the conductor were still standing.

The conductor snapped the cover closed on his watch, then waved toward the engine. The engineer blew the whistle twice, then opened the throttle. The conductor stepped up on to the train just as it began to roll.

"If you see the station master, tell him we couldn't wait," the conductor called back to Hawke as the train began gathering speed. "You folks have a real nice visit."

"Thanks," Rachel called back to him.

Hawke and Rachel stood on the depot platform until the train reached the edge of town. The sound of the train receded in the distance, to be replaced by the high keening moan of a prairie wind. A dust devil danced across the street and a sign that read HARDWARE, TINWARE, AND NOTIONS squeaked as it was jerked back and forth by the force of the wind. Somewhere a dog barked.

"Let's go into the depot and see if anyone is here," Hawke suggested.

They went into the depot and looked around but saw nobody.

"Hello?" Hawke called.

When he didn't get an answer, Hawke walked around behind the ticket counter but found the area completely deserted. He checked two of the side rooms and found them empty as well.

From another part of the building, the telegraph started clacking and the sudden intrusion of sound in the abandoned building startled both of them.

"Maybe the telegrapher knows what's going on," Hawke said, starting toward the sound. He opened the door and looked in, but no one was in the room.

The clacking of the telegraph was from a signal being received at the other end. Hawke could not read telegraphy, but as a musician he was keenly attuned to rhythm. As the same rhythmic pattern kept repeating itself, he had the opinion that some distant telegrapher was trying to get the attention of the Bellefont station.

"I wonder where everyone is," Rachel said.

"Well, if it's just a one-man operation, the way the conductor said, maybe he's not feeling very well. It's not like he has a rush of business," Hawke said.

Rachel chuckled. "You've got that right." She looked toward the clock, then turned her head quizzically. The clock read: 11:28. The pendulum was hanging motionless in the glass-fronted case.

"Mason, look at the clock. It's about five hours late."

Hawke walked over to the clock and started the pendulum. It moved back and forth enough times to indicate there was nothing wrong with the clock.

"It's run down," Hawke said in surprise. "Why would you let a clock run down in a railroad depot? Of all places, you would think a train station would need to have an accurate timepiece."

"What do we do now?"

"Do you know where your friend Louise lives?"

"No," Rachel said. "I just send the mail to her in care of general delivery, Bellefont. But I did send her a telegram telling her that I would be arriving today. I'm a little surprised that she isn't here to meet us."

"It shouldn't be all that hard to find her. Look at that sign."

WELCOME TO

BELLEFONT

POPULATION: 103

"With a population like that, I suspect everyone in town will know her."

"It isn't a very big town, is it? Unless everybody in town gambles, I don't know where I'm going to get my business."

"I wouldn't worry about that," Hawke replied. "These small Western towns generally get most of their business from the ranches and farms around it. You'll be surprised at how much business you'll have." He picked up the two suitcases. "There's the hotel across the street. What do you say we go get checked in? Then we can walk down to your friend's store."

"Sounds like a good idea," Rachel said as she started toward the Railroad Hotel with him.

As they crossed the street, they heard a cow bawling.

"What's that?" Rachel asked.

Hawke laughed. "Don't tell me the Brubaker Farm didn't have cows," he teased. "She just needs milking. That's all."

"Of course we had cows, but I didn't do such things. I was a pampered Southern Belle, remember?"

Another cow joined the first.

"Sounds like another cow needs milking," Rachel said.

They stepped up on to the porch of the hotel, then Hawke pushed the door open and they went inside. There was nobody behind the desk.

"Hello?" Hawke called. His call got no response.

They looked around the lobby of the hotel. It had two overstuffed chairs, a spittoon, a small table, and a dark blue carpet on the floor.

"Mason, look. This clock has stopped too."

"Maybe the clerk is asleep," Hawke suggested. He leaned over the check-in desk but saw no one.

"I guess they don't want our business," Rachel said.

"Well, they're going to get our business, whether they want it or not," Hawke said. Behind the counter he saw a big board of keys. From some of the hooks only one key hung; from others, two keys were hanging. He selected keys from a couple of the hooks that had two keys each.

"You'll be in Room 23, I'll be in Room 24," he said, handing her a key. He turned the registration book around and started to sign it but paused when he saw one of the names.

"Rachel, Tangeleno and Vizzini are here," Hawke said quietly.

Rachel gasped. "Here? In this hotel?"

"Yes," Hawke said. "One is in Room 22, the other is in Room 28."

Even as Hawke was identifying the room, he took the spare keys for rooms 22 and 28 down from the board. Then he pulled his pistol and spun the cylinder, checking the loads. "It looks like this time we have the upper hand."

"What are you going to do?" she asked.

"I'm going to kill them," Hawke said easily.

With his pistol in hand, Hawke crossed the lobby and climbed the steps. Reaching the second floor, he heard a slapping sound from the far end of the hall and he spun quickly, cocking his pistol and bringing it up as he did so.

The sound came from the open window at the far end of the hall. Wind was blowing against a windowshade, lifting it away from the window when the breeze was strong enough, letting it fall back as the wind waned.

Chastising himself for being so jumpy, Hawke continued to walk down the hallway. He stepped as close to the wall as he could because he knew that the floorboards would be less likely to squeak or strain there.

Moving very quietly, he reached Room 22 and stopped just outside the door. He put his ear to the door and listened to see if he could hear any sound that would indicate there was someone in the room.

Hearing nothing, he put the key in the lock, turned it, then stepped back out of the way, expecting a fusillade of shots to come through the door.

No shots were fired.

With his weapon drawn, Hawke dived into the room. He rolled once, then came up with his gun cocked and pointing at the bed.

The bed was empty.

Quickly, Hawke looked all the way around the room.

Like the bed, the room was empty.

Hawke backed out into the hallway, then started trying other doors. Not one door was locked—and not one room was occupied.

•

He went back downstairs.

"Rachel?"

Rachel rose up from behind the desk. "What happened?" she asked.

"Nothing. The rooms were empty. The entire hotel is empty."

"The *hotel* is empty," Rachel said. "If you ask me, this entire *town* is empty. We haven't seen a living soul since we got off the train. I don't mind telling you, I'm beginning to find this whole thing rather creepy."

"It does seem a little odd," Hawke agreed. Hawke walked over to the front window and looked out onto the main street of Bellefont.

"Do you see anyone out there?" Rachel asked.

"No, not a soul. What's the name of your friend's store?"

"Smalley's."

"Let's go find it."

"All right. Anything is better than hanging around in this mausoleum," Rachel agreed.

It wasn't hard to find the store. It was right next door to the hotel. From the outside it looked as deserted as the street, but when Rachel tried the doorknob, she found that it was unlocked.

"Oh, good, it's open," she said with a broad smile. The little bell on the door rang cheerily as Rachel pushed it open.

"Louise!" Rachel called. "Louise, it's me, Rachel!"

No one responded to the call.

"Now, don't tell me there's nobody here either," Rachel said in frustration. "That doesn't make any sense. Why would they leave the store completely unlocked if there is nobody here?"

The Reverend Timothy Gadbury looked at the eleven children who were tied together in the sanctuary of the church.

They had been here since early morning and the children, as well as the people of the town, were exhausted.

At least they weren't starving—or dying for lack of water. Tangeleno had allowed some of the women to leave the church long enough to prepare food and bring water for everyone. But he chose only the mothers of the children so he could be sure they would come back.

Looking around the room, Gadbury saw that Vizzini was sitting in a chair near the altar with a shotgun across his lap. All through the day, he had held the gun pressed against one or another of the children.

At one point just after lunch, when it was obvious that Vizzini was nodding off, a couple of the men were contemplating jumping him.

"No," Gadbury had told them. "Look at the way he is holding that gun. The least disturbance could cause it to go off."

"We'll grab the gun first."

"It's too risky. Even if you got his gun, you would still have the other one to contend with."

"You'd better listen to the preacher, gentlemen," Tangeleno said.

The men gasped in surprise, for they had not heard Tangeleno sneak up on them. After that, no further plans to overcome their guards were contemplated.

Gadbury heard the train arrive, then depart.

"The train is here," he said.

"Yes," Tangeleno replied.

"How long are you going to keep us?" Reverend Gadbury asked. "You said you would let us go when the train arrived. Well, the train has arrived."

"I said, also, that I was going to keep you as long as it takes," Tangeleno said.

"Then, in God's name, please let the children go. They can do you no harm."

Tangeleno shook his head. "I can't let them go. They're my insurance. The only way I can keep the entire town locked up in this church is because they know that if one citizen of this town leaves the church . . . even one . . . I will kill one of the children."

"That is unconscionable, sir," the reverend said. "Not even a seed of Satan can be that evil."

"Why, didn't you know, Padre?" Tangeleno replied. "I *am* the seed of Satan." He laughed.

"I offer myself in place of these children."

"Ha!" Tangeleno said. "Do you really think anyone in this town gives one damn about whether you live or die? Thank you for your offer, Padre, but I'll stick with the children."

"Hey, Eddie," one of the men called. "Looks like you've got some customers in your store."

"Impossible," Eddie said. "Everyone in town is right here in the church."

"Yeah, well, they aren't from town," the man said. "It's a man and a woman and I ain't never seen either one before."

"Take a look, Vizzini," Tangeleno said.

Vizzini walked over to the window and looked through it.

"Yeah, it's them," he said.

Tangeleno looked at Louise. "Go invite Rachel to come to church," he said. "Not the man with her. I want him to remain in the hotel. Just bring Rachel."

Louise shook her head no. "You want me to invite my friend down here so you can kill her? No, I won't do it."

In a sudden and unexpected move, Tangeleno slashed his knife across the Reverend Gadbury's throat. With a look of total shock and fear, Gadbury put his hands to his neck, but could do nothing to stop the fountain of blood that gurgled through his hands. His eyes rolled up in his head and he fell backward, lay on the floor kicking his left leg rather convulsively for a moment, then died.

It all happened so fast that no one had the opportunity to scream—or even call out.

"Now, Louise, I'm going to ask you again to go down there and invite your friend to join us," Tangeleno said. "If you refuse again, I'll kill one of the children, just the way I killed the preacher."

"All right, all right, I'll go," Louise said.

"Now, do you see what you have done, Louise? If you had been more cooperative in the beginning, poor Reverend Gadbury would still be alive. It's all your fault."

"I'm sorry," Louis said, weeping now.

"It's not your fault, Mrs. Smalley. You didn't kill Reverend Gadbury. He did," Betty said, glaring bitterly at Tangeleno.

"Folks!" Tangeleno said. "Trust me, this is soon going to be all over. Then I'll let you all go about your business. But if you do not do exactly what I tell you to do, I will kill one of the children, and then one of you, until I get my way. Is that clearly understood by all?"

Some of the adults were wearing expressions of fear, others embittered rage, while still others were so exhausted from their ordeal that it was all they could do to stay alert.

"If I go get her for you, will you let everyone go?" Louise asked.

"If you don't do it for me, I will kill two of the children, then your husband," Tangeleno said.

"Louise, go, please go!" Betty said.

Louise waited for a moment, then nodded. "All right," she said. "I'll go."

"I just saw them go back into the hotel," Ely said from the front of the church.

Louise nodded, then stepped out of the door and started up the street toward the hotel.

"Don Tangeleno, you think we should leave Hawke back in the hotel by himself?" Vizzini asked.

"If we have the whore, we'll have the advantage," Tangeleno said. "We can force him to come down—without his gun."

Chapter 34

WHEN HAWKE AND RACHEL RETURNED TO THE hotel, Hawke shook his head. "There is something going on here," he said. "An entire town doesn't just disappear."

"I'm frightened," Rachel said.

Hawke laughed. "We've come halfway across the country with half a dozen attempts to kill you and you take that fine. But we get to a town where there is nobody home and that frightens you."

"You said yourself that something was going on, that an entire town doesn't . . ."

The front door opened and Hawke whirled toward it, drawing as he turned so that when the woman stepped into the hotel lobby, she was staring down the barrel of Hawke's gun.

"No!" she said, throwing her hands up.

"No, don't shoot, Mason! It's Louise!" Rachel shouted, though her warning wasn't necessary, for Hawke had already lowered his pistol.

"Hello, Rachel," Louise said.

"Mason, this is Louise. Louise, this is my friend, Mason Hawke."

"Mr. Hawke," Louise said with a slight nod.

"Louise, what is going on in this town? Where is everyone?" Rachel asked.

"They are all in church."

" 'Church?' The entire town is in church? You must have some kind of a preacher," Hawke said with a little chuckle.

"No, it's not like that," Louise replied. She looked at Rachel. "Rachel, he wants you to come with me." She looked at Hawke. "But not you. Just Rachel."

"Who wants me to . . ." Rachel started, then she gasped and put her hand to her mouth. "Oh my God, it's Tangeleno, isn't it?"

"Yes," Louise said. "He and Vizzini are holding the entire town captive in the church. He says if I don't come back with you, he will start killing the children."

" 'Children'? What children?" Rachel asked.

"The children of the town," Louise said. "That's how he managed to keep us all locked up in the church until you got here. He threatened to kill the children if anyone tried to leave. He's already killed two people, including the preacher."

"You go back and tell Tangeleno if he wants to see her, he can come down here," Hawke said.

"Please, Mr. Hawke," Louise begged. "If you have ever stared into the face of pure evil, it is this man. He will kill Eddie and as many of the children as it takes to get Rachel to come down there."

"I'm going, Mason," Rachel said resolutely.

"All right. But if you go, I'm going with you."

"No, please don't," Louise said. "Tangeleno said to bring Rachel alone. He was very insistent about that."

"I am not going to let her . . ."

"I'm going, Mason," Rachel said again, more resolutely this time. "I'm not going to be responsible for the death of innocent children."

Hawke looked at her for a long moment, knowing that he couldn't talk her out of it, knowing that he wouldn't prevent it. He sighed, then nodded.

Rachel swallowed, then nodded back at him. She looked over at Louise. "All right, let's go," she said.

"Thank you," Louise replied gratefully.

As soon as Rachel and Louise stepped outside, Hawke moved to the window of the hotel. He looked down the long street toward the church, which anchored the far end of town. He saw Tangeleno and Vizzini came out into the street then. Vizzini had a young girl with him, and his right arm was in front of her, holding a shotgun, with the barrel of the gun just under her chin.

Hawke felt an intense sense of frustration. He had no intention of standing here and watching Vizzini kill Rachel in cold blood, but he had no idea what he could do to prevent it.

Turning away from the window, he kicked the chair in disgust. That's when he saw Rachel's suitcase, his suitcase, and the little canvas pouch the baggage handler had given him to leave with the hotel clerk. He opened the package and looked at it. It was a knife, but not just any knife. It was, according to the letter accompanying the knife: "An extraordinary throwing knife, handcrafted by the master knife maker Thomas Turner of Sheffield, England.

Hawke picked up the knife. He had never held one more perfectly balanced.

"Hawke!" It was a man's voice, calling him from the street outside. "Hawke, come on out!"

Hawke slipped the knife into his belt, behind him, then walked outside.

Tangeleno and Vizzini were standing in the middle of the street. By now, Vizzini had let the little girl go and was holding a shotgun against Rachel's head. Tangeleno was standing beside him. The townspeople, freed now, were running to get out of the way.

"You see that horse trough there just in front of you?" Tangeleno called.

"I see it," Hawke answered.

"I want you to take your gun out, real slow, and drop it in the water."

Hawke hesitated for a moment.

"Do it or I'll have Vizzini blow this whore's brains out," Tangeleno ordered.

Hawke started for his gun.

"Use your thumb and finger," Tangeleno said.

Complying with the demand, Hawke used just his thumb and forefinger to extract the pistol. Then, holding it in such a fashion, he carried it over to the water trough and dropped it in.

Tangeleno laughed.

"Now you can come closer," he said.

Hawke started up the street toward Tangeleno, Vizzini, and Rachel.

"You are a hard man to kill, piano player," Tangeleno said.

"I try to be," Hawke said. He continued to move toward them.

"I don't know how many of my men I've sent after you. And every one of them failed. So, I guess I'll just have to do the job myself."

"Not all by yourself," Hawke said. "I see you've got your lackey with you." He nodded toward Vizzini.

"Oh, don't worry about him. I'm going to let him kill the whore. I'll take care of you."

"It figures you'd let Vizzini kill the woman. He likes to hurt women, don't you, Vizzini?"

Vizzini chuckled. "If you had been anything more than a whorehouse piano player, you would know that sometimes you've got to show a woman who is the boss."

"Tell me, Vizzini, after I threw you in the toilet that night, how long did it take you to get the shit washed off?"

"What? Do you expect me to believe that you are the one who did that?"

"What was it I called you that night?" Hawke asked. "I believe I called you a piece of shit."

For just a moment, Vizzini thought back to that night and he remembered the words vividly.

"What?" he sputtered. "It was you, you son of a bitch!" Vizzini shouted loudly. Angrily, he pushed Rachel away, so he could bring his shotgun to bear on Hawke, which was exactly what Hawke wanted him to do.

"Vizzini, no! What are you doing?" Tangeleno shouted, totally in the dark as to what had just made Vizzini so angry.

As Vizzini brought his gun around, Hawke pulled the knife from his belt in the back, then whipped his arm in a throwing motion. The handcrafted Sheffield blade flipped over once, then flew unerringly to Vizzini, hitting him in the middle of the forehead and burying itself deep into his brain. Vizzini fell back, dead before he even hit the ground.

"No!" Tangeleno shouted in shock and anger over what had just happened. He fired one barrel of his shotgun toward Hawke, but even as he was pulling the trigger, Hawke was diving toward Vizzini. Three of the pellets hit Hawke's right calf muscle, the rest of them sped by.

Hawke landed on top of Vizzini, then grabbed his shotgun and rolled over once, as Tangeleno, trying to correct, swung toward him. Tangeleno didn't manage to pull the trigger the second time, because Hawke fired both barrels at the same time. The double-charge, this close, blew half of Tangeleno's head away.

Epilogue

IT WAS SAID OF THE QUEEN OF HEARTS, THAT
Rachel Brabaker ran honest games, served free liquor to the
players, and maintained a gambling establishment of style
and class. The latter was due in part to Hawke's piano playing, where it was said that saloon ditties would never be
heard.

The reputation of the Queen of Hearts grew so that it drew
gamblers, by the train load from as faraway as St. Louis and
Denver.

Hawke stayed on for almost four months, long after he had
healed from the three shotgun pellets, until he was certain
that Rachel was no longer in danger. He might have stayed
just a little longer if Rachel had not started hinting that there
was a way Hawke could make his stay permanent.

It was the quiet predawn dark of early morning when Hawke
went down to the stable to saddle his horse. He had told
Rachel that he would be leaving soon, though without being
specific as to when.

Hawke was a brave man who would face, without fear, any

adversary. But he did not want to have to tell Rachel that the plans she was making for him were not the plans he had for himself. That's why he went to bed the night before, with absolutely no hint that he would be leaving the next morning.

Hawke and his horse, a new mount that he had bought within the past two weeks, blew clouds of vapor that drifted away in feathery wisps in the cold morning air. A breeze came up, colder than it had been, and he knew that the long lingering days of a warm fall were about over. It would be winter soon, and snow would be covering the plains.

Hawke swung into his saddle and rode out of town, heading south. He had never cared much for the cold.